D1058441

FORBIDDEN

FORBIDDEN

JUDY WAITE

ATHENEUM BOOKS FOR YOUNG READERS
New York London Toronto Sydney

ATHENEUM BOOKS FOR YOUNG READERS
An imprint of Simon & Schuster Children's Publishing Division
1230 Avenue of the Americas, New York, New York 10020
First published in England in 2004 by Oxford University Press
First U. S. edition 2006
Book design by Yaffa Jaskoll
The text for this book is set in Aldine721 BT.
Manufactured in the United States of America
10 9 8 7 6 5 4 3 2 1
Library of Congress Cataloging-in-Publication Data
Waite, Judy.
Forbidden / Judy Waite.—1st ed.
p. cm.
Summary: Elinor has lived in a cult her entire life, but when she meets a boy who looks strangely familiar, she begins to question what she has been taught.
ISBN-13: 978-0-689-87642-4
ISBN-10: 0-689-87642-4
[1. Cults—Fiction.] I. Title.
PZ7.W13325Fo 2006
[Fic]—dc22   2004027898

For Libby

PART ONE

1

I am getting Bad Thoughts.

I must push them away and try to concentrate. Concentrate.

Fog has thickened the air and turned us ghosted and grey. Isabel presses close to me as we gather in the Hill Park grounds with the other Followers. It is not easy to see Meryl through the haze.

Two Watchers lead her out from the back of the van and over to one of the trees. The tree has been lopped back to make stubbed shapes, like all the others inside the grounds. Meryl stumbles between the Watchers and they hold her as she tries to walk, her bare feet dragging a ragged line across the frosted grass. They have shaved her hair and it shocks me. Meryl's hair was spun gold and spilled like a waterfall down her back. We have to keep our hair long and loose, because Howard likes it like that. Or at least he likes it on us. His Chosen. The ordinary Followers do not matter. Without her hair Meryl looks lost, and I wish I could turn back time and make everything all right. I was her Shadow on the streets. She taught me things. Kept me safe. But these are Bad Thoughts again and I have to stop remembering. What is happening is necessary.

Necessary.

The word saws into me, splintering off the Bad Thoughts and leaving only the truth. Necessary. Necessary.

They reach the tree and one of the Watchers turns Meryl so her back is to us. She is wearing a thin beige dress that blends with her skin, and the whole look of her now seems to belong in the strange blurred morning.

I wonder if she is cold.

The Watchers work fast, strapping her wrists onto heavy metal rings that are banded on to the trunk.

"Elinor?" Isabel touches my hand. "Will Meryl be all right?"

"She has to Receive Punishment. There is no choice." I put my arm round Isabel's shoulder and am startled by how thin she is. I hope she is not ill. Getting ill is a Bad Thing. There is no time for getting ill.

I start to chant, my lips shaping soundlessly, "True Cause is the true cause. True Cause is the true cause." Or at least I think it is soundless, but now others are joining in and Followers are linking arms, pressing closer together, and we are all feeling the warmth and comfort flow into each other. I sway slightly, giddy with the rush of love, and in the giddiness there floats the sudden question of what it is like to Betray. Betray. A twisted black damage word. A word to describe what Meryl has done.

"True Cause is the true cause. True Cause is the true cause."

The chant seems to muffle up inside the fog and hang there so that I am not sure if we are all still speaking or if the words have got trapped somehow and are just echoing back.

I am drifting.

Suddenly two lights pour cold beams down the drive from the mansion, and I make my eyes focus on them as they glide towards us. It is Howard's white limousine, the fog curling like breath in its headlamps.

Rael, Howard's Chief Watcher, opens the passenger

door and Howard gets out. Silver blond. Wire limbed. His amazing eyes deep-set and black as coals. He faces us and everything about him seems to buzz and crackle as if he is lit from the inside. Our mood ignites like a spark on tired ashes. I become elated, just looking at him. I can never watch him enough. Never be near him enough. He walks across to where Meryl is tied, then stops, pressing his fingers against the W that scars his forehead. I think he must be sending her a message with his mind. Some words of warmth. Even when he is angry, Howard can always find room to love.

We are lucky. So lucky.

Howard raises both hands and our chant fades, although some of us are still swaying very slightly. I can feel my face smiling and I am filled with a sweet calm.

Everything will be all right.

Everything will be all right.

He does not speak to Meryl. I had thought he might—maybe touch her or talk to her or something. In another month, on her sixteenth birthday, she would have been Bonded to him. But perhaps he cannot bear it that she has wandered from the Path. I am not able to make out the detail of his face but I am sure that grief will be burnt across it. Howard feels everything. When he stands still he can feel the grass grow.

What is happening to Meryl is necessary. Necessary. True Cause is the true cause. Howard holds a rope in his hand. I think he must be going to be the one to use it, but Rael strides over and takes it. He fixes Meryl with his milk-pale stare and swishes the rope, grazing the air.

Meryl's shoulders flinch and I think of a deer we startled in the woods last week. Meryl and me out collecting leaves and cones to dry for the potpourri baskets. The deer flinched like that before it ran. Only Meryl's hands are tied and the rope is raised and she cannot run.

Howard nods.

Rael raises his hand.

I tighten my arm around Isabel.

True Cause is the true cause. Necessary. Necessary.

I do not want to look. Instead I stare down at where the ground has seeped a damp stain over the toes of my leather boots. Meryl must know that this is for her own good. For the good of all of us.

True Cause is the true cause. Necessary. Necessary.

A gasp from the Followers stirs me, and I look

up. Howard has moved between Rael and Meryl.

Howard our Master.

Howard who Saves.

Rael twists sideways and the rope misses Meryl and whips the tree. Splinters of bark spit and fall. A curved weal gashes a scar down the trunk.

Now Howard is facing us again, his head up and thrown back slightly. I feel the burn of his stare. I feel the moment when his look singes mine. I feel the fire of everything he knows.

We stand, all of us trembling and sorry, as if it was us and not Meryl who gave herself to an Outsider.

Isabel is crying.

Howard looks at her, and then at me with my arm around her.

My knees weaken under the weight of his gaze. Tie me up. Punish me. I am sorry. So sorry.

I know—have always known—that there is something different in the way Howard looks at me. He whispered once that my eyes and my hair drew me to him. I was puzzled at the time, but Meryl thought it was probably because I have a look like his. Black, slant-shaped eyes and silvery blonde hair. I do not think of this often, because of course vanity is a Bad Thing. The outer form is nothing and nowhere. We learn to love the soul within. But still sometimes I am glad that I have a look that pleases him.

Howard brings me back to the moment. He lifts his arms and I have the idea he is about to shout. Even roar. But instead he stares beyond us, as if he is scanning the bushes and trees. "There are Outsiders who want to destroy our Cause. They are dangerous, and devious. Trust leads to tragedy. We must be watchful. We must be wary." Then, bringing his gaze back on to us, "This day is your warning. Learn from it."

Nobody moves. Nobody breathes.

The cold threat ices up our bones, and we are locked where we stand.

And then Howard smiles.

The fear melts. I smile back at him. Everybody does.

Howard takes Rael's hand, and nods at the other two Watchers, who have been waiting by the van. Stepping forward as if they are all just acting out one of our Role Play Programmes, they untie Meryl and turn her round. "I know this has seemed rough," Howard gathers her to him, and his voice is a soft caress, "but sometimes I have to make hard choices—I need to find ways to hammer these messages home. If we can't stay in line with each other now, how will we handle Endtime together? You do understand?"

I expect her to hold on to him. To thank him even. Howard is right—there are terrible things coming. He is only trying to save us. But Meryl is not looking thankful. Her eyes are dead and empty, and she looks as though she does not care. I know then that it is not just the hair. Something deep in the centre of Meryl has been cut away. How can that have happened? She grew up with me. With all of us. We are Howard's Chosen. When Endtime comes we will be the New Beginning.

I keep watching her. She changed slowly, I suppose. Struggling to think back, I pull out fuzzed memories of times when she slipped away from me. Questions she asked that seemed edged with Bad Thoughts. I never tried to fit these things together. I never understood that I needed to. Did I let her down?

Isabel starts to swing my arm as if she wants to dance. She hugs me and now everyone is hugging and saying they knew he would not do it. But he had to warn us. True Cause is the true cause. Necessary. Necessary.

I hug everyone back.

"I love you," they say.

"Love you."

"Love you."

"I love you too," I reply. But a part of me is not with them.

I feel queasy. Uneasy. Outsiders can be dangerous and devious. Trust leads to tragedy. So surely Meryl has been abused? Might we not all have helped her more through love, not fear? I feel suddenly as if I am a deer that has stupidly strayed from the safety of the herd, and although it has lived in the same woods all its life, it is suddenly not certain of exactly where it is standing.

2

I should not be tramping towards these woods on my own.

Isabel is my new Shadow now—they teamed Laura together with Sarah and Gabriella to free her for me—and we are supposed to watch out for each other. We should never be apart.

I have lied to get away like this—pretended I am going to an Unburdening—and the lie has scared me. I never lie. None of us do. There is nothing for us to lie about. But Rael had brought Howard's most recent Divine Writings to the School Room, and we were scribing the updates in The Book, titling it:

WHY ARE WE HERE?

when Isabel started humming one of the True Cause hymns. The tune stabbed in my head, and I suddenly had to try and blot it away, so I said, "What do you think has happened to Meryl?" The words spilled without me even knowing I was going to say them, smearing the air between us. There are eleven of us Chosen now, and even though there are no Watchers in our shed at the end of each day, nobody has mentioned Meryl since the black van drove her away.

"I don't know." Isabel leant closer over her work and her humming got louder. I knew I had said a Bad Thing, but the question was still swilling round in me.

I tried to keep focused on my writing, but everything became blotched and blurred, and then the idea of the lie came. I placed my pen back in the pot. "I think I need to Unburden!" I got up slowly and walked towards the door.

Isabel just kept humming, and did not even look round.

And now I am here—heading for the trees.

It is foggy again. The mud makes for heavy going and I have to lift my Tuesday dress because I do not want to dirty the hem. The cloth is brown so the mud should blend in, but I cannot take risks.

I pass near the gate that guards Hill Park. The mansion is obscured beneath the fog, but I am terrified that one of the Watchers might loom up out of the grey grounds and demand to know why I am out without my Shadow.

What would I say? Except that I cannot get Meryl out of my head. She has been there all week, through the meetings and the meditations and the Prediction Practice Programmes that, woven amongst our school work, fill most of our days.

Is Meryl a Bad Thought? I am not sure. But I cannot—dare not—Unburden and find out. Counsellors have to pass on our Unburdenings to Howard, and I know my struggle will bring him new pain.

So I will try walking with the memory of her in the woods, and I have an idea that I can maybe ask her to go, the way we ask other Bad Thoughts to go in the weekly Cleansings. I run a little, trying to keep my breathing steady. The rasping of breath may be easy to hear.

Reaching the edge of the wood I pick my way through the straggled holly. We gather it each Christmas. Not our Christmas, of course. Christmas is an evil time. An Outsider time. It dazzles them, and it deadens them. But we make good money from the holly.

The path twists deeper and I stop, resting my head against an ancient oak. Howard says that when he walks alone he hears the trees speak. It seems probable to me that trees will have deep creaking voices and sometimes I try to pick up their words, pressing my ears against the rough bark. It has never worked before, but maybe I should try it now. Maybe the trees will creak me some answers.

I press my forehead hard against the trunk and wait for great wisdom. Everything falls still. Even the rooks stop calling. I try to believe that this silence is a sign and my heart beats faster. I want this to happen. I want this tree to make everything all right.

"Hi."

I jolt, struggling with the shock that the voice is not at all treelike. And then I realize that it was not the tree that spoke, but someone behind me. I turn and see a stranger. He is my age—maybe a few years older—and not in Tuesday browns. An Outsider.

I straighten my shoulders, my own voice spiked and suspicious. "What are you doing here? This land is private."

He looks awkward for a moment, and then shrugs. "I was driving about—I've just passed my test and Dad bought me a banger to get about in. I reckoned these woods looked interesting, so I parked up on the verge." He waves a notebook at me. "I know it sounds pretty geeky, but I was looking for inspiration and I guess I just couldn't resist it."

I do not understand about tests and bangers. I do not know what geeky means. But Inspiration is a big part of Prediction Practice and I am always struggling to develop it.

"Inspiration for what?" I tilt my head slightly to try and see on to the open page of his notebook.

He closes it quickly and looks uncomfortable again. "I've just been scribbling down a few ideas. My mates reckon I'm soft and should be out kicking a ball across a muddy field but . . ." He shrugs, and then smiles.

I stare at him. He looks untidy—mud on his jacket and scratches on one side of his face. I think I should run. Run away through the trees and the mud, screaming all the way back to Howard's gates and calling all the Watchers and Rael and maybe even Howard too. Our fences are high and barbed. No one should get in.

But as I look across at him the panic shrivels and all I can think is that his eyes are moss-green and very warm. The warmth. That is the thing about them. And it scares me.

"I'm not a nutter or anything." His voice is warm too. "Are you . . . okay?"

"Why wouldn't I be?"

"I just—I wondered why you'd come out here on your own and stuff. I thought you might be having some sort of problem. If you are, I could try and help."

I step back, almost snagging with the holly. Something scratches at my memory that I cannot break the surface of, but I know that its roots run back to the time when Howard first made me one of his Chosen. A Bad Thing happened then. If I forget to concentrate on True Cause properly, the Image crowds in from the dark at the back of my mind. There is a room. A woman crying. A man's voice urging, "Think for yourself, Maria. Think for yourself."

I realize I am staring at the Outsider. There is something in the set of his face, the shape of his mouth, the line of his cheek, that is unsettling me. I cannot explain it, but it hurts. I suddenly have the sense of losing something that I have never even found.

I think I should bring True Cause to him—help him to be saved—but then the memory of Meryl presses in and my head starts stabbing again. "I'm going." All at once I feel tired, as if something has flashed up and then frizzled away, burning me out. "You should go too. If the Watchers find you here . . ."

I trail off. I should not warn him. I should let the Watchers do what they have to do. True Cause is the true cause. Necessary. Necessary.

He shrugs, then smiles. "Take care," he says. That warmth again. I shiver.

Turning sharply, I push back out into the day.

The fog has thinned and I can see the white stone of Hill Park mansion and I make myself grateful that I belong to Howard's world. I am lucky. So lucky.

I will go straight to a Counsellor and Unburden everything that has just happened. The Watchers will check the grounds. If the Outsider is still about, they will find him.

I head for the farm and see the other Chosen hurrying to greet the New Joiner arrivals. Ten girls in brown dresses linking arms and singing as they walk. I run like a child, my skirt hitched up to stop myself from tripping. I want to get back to where everything is safe. Lucky. So lucky. True Cause is the true cause.

Only, as I run, I have to pass the tree that Meryl was tied to. It is behind the railed fence that separates the grounds from the farm, but through the gaps I can see that the metal bands are still strapped to the trunk.

I stop. A straggle of crows rises up from the stubbed branches, their cries achingly sad.

Where is Meryl now?

I walk on quickly. I must not think. Must not think. But seeping from under the block that I am nailing in my head is the sudden knowledge that I will not Unburden about the Outsider in the woods.

3

"It began with a vision. Although it was not just a vision . . ."

Rael opens the door to the chamber and Howard bursts through, his voice ringing out the familiar words as he strides to the front of Star Temple, his white robe shimmering.

I watch from the raised floor that has been built on either side. The raised floor is only for the Chosen, and a line of candles flickers round us and throws out tiny breaths of heat.

Howard had first fixed his stare on the New Joiners who make up the front two rows, but now his eyes sweep the crush of Base Level Followers, the smaller groups of Intermediates and High Orders, and finally us Chosen. It is a brief, fierce look, but in it we are all connected.

I am usually living for this moment—the time when his look sparks against mine—but today I am unsettled.

Moss-green eyes. Take care. Take care.

I grip Isabel's hand so tightly that she leans nearer and whispers, "Are you all right?"

"Yes, of course." I have to concentrate. Concentrate.

I struggle to feel the power that always pours from Howard when he unfolds his Vision. "I was young," he says. "Not then twenty. But my heart was already heavy. Weary. As if all the best songs were already sung . . ."

His words roll across me.

I have heard them for so long—I am not sure how many years—but it is as if they are part of me. I have been shaped by them. They make patterns that I can slot into without even knowing it has happened.

My mind drifts to the time last year when we built Star Temple. It took seven weeks, working through the burn of summer.

There was an outcry about the temple from Outsiders in Braxbury, but men in suits came and

Howard seems to have satisfied their complaints. One is a Follower now. When the gold-domed roof was finally finished the day flowed into a night of celebration. There was dancing and singing and biscuits baked in the shape of stars. When all the wildness and the eating was done, I stood watching the final splutter of fireworks in the darkness and Howard had, for the briefest moment, touched my breast. "It's a torture, waiting for you," he whispered.

My face burns now at the memory, but I keep my eyes on him as he stands, hands clenched, and sweeps us with another look of fire.

I clench my hands, in line with the rest of the Chosen. The Followers clench their hands too, and a moment later New Joiners join in as they suddenly understand Howard's unspoken cue.

It never takes long for New Joiners to learn. Not those who are listening. Those who are ready.

Howard's voice rises. "On this day—the day of the vision—I had walked to a strange town, then struggled up a hill. I was hoping for what peace the view might bring. Hoping for something to make me sing . . ."

As his voice drops back again I can hear tiny flutterings from the candles. ". . . . but no song came.

Instead I saw the small town crouched and grey. Huddled houses. Hurrying people. Just to see them crippled me with pain."

For some time after the celebration I would tremble when Howard was near. What if I was suddenly Called? It would be early—too early—and anyway it had to be Meryl before me, but I Imaged a fantasy that Howard might have been commanded by the Divine Writings to change the True Cause order. It was possible. And I hoped.

"I was desolate . . ." Howard's robe flows behind him as he descends the tiled steps, each tile decorated with the True Cause star, ". . . and wondering how it was that all mankind could only seem to seek, but never find . . ."

I begin tracing a small scar on the edge of my thumb. The Chosen—all of us—prepared the painted glass for the arched window that now spills light into the temple, throwing more star patterns across the faces of the New Joiners. We grew so tired, working when the base level and intermediate Followers slept, but the window was a Glorious Thing and it was an honour for us to be selected to do it. I had a mass of cuts and burns from where my mind—and hands—sometimes slipped as I worked, but I was happy. So happy. The end always justifies the means.

Howard reaches the back of the temple and, stretching both arms as if he is a giant bird, drops his head. "There was deadness in me, like a great grey rat lying lifeless in the gutter. I could only shake my head and mutter that we might all be better dead . . ."

We drop our heads and whisper, "Better dead. Better dead."

Howard is walking back again and shouting, "And then I thought that it was such a desperate thing I'd said. And I cried, still wishing I had died."

We all enter the State of Sorrow. This is a silent grief that seeps water from our eyes and always gives me the taste of salt upon my lips. I do not know if the salt is tasted by the other Chosen because I have never asked them. I have never thought to.

Howard pauses. He always pauses here. When I was younger I used to count . . . thirteen . . . fourteen . . . fifteen. The gap was always the same. Fifteen. I could never get to sixteen.

He starts up again. "Then darkness made a cloak that fell upon the throat of the town. And all the stars were falling. Falling down . . ."

Howard mounts the steps to the platform.

The candles that surround us snuff out, and Watchers roll down the black blinds to block the light from the windows. Howard's voice curls through the dark. ". . . I realized I was kneeling . . ."

I can see his shadowed shape bend and kneel.

All our shadowed shapes bend and kneel.

". . . And through the black a streak of angry fire curled and spat, its wild flames reaching higher. And all around was crashing . . ."

A flame flashes suddenly from just behind him, streaking gold and lighting him as if he himself is the vision.

There are gasps of panic from the New Joiners.

". . . I heard buildings falling. Trapped men calling." His voice drops slow and low, but I know that even at the back they can all still hear him whisper. "I knew that evil danced down there . . ."

We begin to moan softly.

Another pause. Another count. Thirteen . . . fourteen . . . fifteen . . .

His words whip up again. ". . . I couldn't just stand still and stare. And so I ran. Though not away, but down. I raced in torment to that tortured town."

The shadow that is Howard stands. We all stand. My knees have gone numb on the hard tiles.

Howard has stretched out his arms again. "Between the ruins curled clouds of dust. There were bodies locked in charred black lust. All passion burnt. No new loves learnt. And . . ." I know he has opened his eyes, for even in the dark he seems to connect with every one of us again. ". . . I reached out to embrace a weeping child."

As he says this he reaches out to the child of a New Joiner—every week there is some new child ready for Howard to choose.

Howard places his hands on the boy's shoulders and hugs him. From the front row a woman with a frizz of yellow hair sinks back to her knees. Her weeping is tumbled up amongst a joyous torrent of thanks.

Watchers thread between us now, passing out lanterns that shine pale white light. Howard faces the New Joiners, still holding the boy tightly.

> "And as we clung I spoke to him in tongues,
> And knew it was that song I hadn't sung.
> And through the song I felt a rushing heat,
> While all the dead rose slowly to their feet.
> And then it came—the thing that I now
>   know—
> My heart lit with a strange but gloried glow.
> And on and on this new light poured from me.
> Its beauty blazed. Its power set me free.
> I knew then with a dazzled certainty . . ."

Thirteen . . . fourteen . . . fifteen . . .

". . . at Endtime the One Saviour would be me."

Howard passes the boy to Rael and steps back, opening his palms and holding his hands out to us. We all stretch our hands back, the New Joiners just seconds behind the rest of us.

I have always been so lifted by this moment. I know that many of the New Joiners will have given themselves up. They are saved. Saved.

"Trust me—follow me," Howard cries. "For it rips my heart to know the price any of you will pay if you don't follow me."

"We follow you, we follow you," we cry back.

But suddenly Meryl is in my head again.

Howard begins chanting, and we all chant too—a soft slow chant that is written with True Cause words—words that only Followers can understand.

I let my mouth form the sounds. *Elinach. Riddulloch. Cant. Neary aw strang. De lintus. De lentus. Mallraoby all fay.*

Around me everyone has closed their eyes. They are swaying. I should do the same, but my eyes stay open, looking round. I am suddenly startled by how our shadows stretch along the temple walls. They dance and flicker like strange demons. I feel a rushing in my head, as if a strong wind is trying to blow me away.

I look to Howard, struggling for reassurance. I do not find it. With his eyes closed and his babble of secret words I think with a cold shock that he looks strange.

I look away, another thought to block, and now my gaze meets and locks, just for a moment, with the milk-pale stare of Rael.

I close my eyes in a sudden panicked hurry to chant and sway.

Take care. Take care.

4

As the girl swings away from the optician's, I step out from the doorway of Woolworth's to talk to her. "Do you have a minute?"

She is young. A bronze-brown suit. Her hair cropped and bottle blonde. I notice her watch is expensive. Gold. We have been trained to look for the smallest detail when we are amongst Outsiders.

She stops and squints. I can see she is puzzling over my Friday dress, but I am used to that.

"Sorry. Too busy. I've just stopped off on my way to work. I shouldn't even be here really." She has a metallic smile. Bronze-brown lipstick on her perfect teeth. She is about to move past me, but I am determined to do a good job. Determined to push away all the Bad Thoughts that have been twining through my head all week. "I just wondered if you'd ever thought about life. What it really means?"

The metallic smile sets even harder. "I gave up on that question a long time ago."

A long time ago.

A long time ago.

The words reach into the dark at the back of my mind, but I block them with a silent True Cause chant. I will blot out all Bad Thoughts. Howard came to us as we were getting ready to leave, and the things he said brought me back to him again. He had received new messages through his Divine Writings. He was in torment, desolate as he broke the news that Endtime is close—closer than even he can bear—and we need to save double the amount of Outsiders each week. Because of this we must Spread the Word without our Shadows, and although this is something new he helped us see that Spreading the Word in towns is safe, and working with Shadows a wicked waste. We do not need our Shadows with us all the time. Sometimes we get abuse when we go house to house, but selling The Book in towns can never hurt us—particularly us Chosen who do not travel so far.

I try to melt the Outsider with my Spread-the-

Word smile. "But that's the tragedy of so many lives. People give up searching. They have everything material, but nothing that really seems to matter."

The Outsider raises her eyebrows, then glances down at her fingers, tutting at a chip in her bronze-brown nails. "Of course things matter. But you're on your own, aren't you? You have to take what you can, and make the best of it."

"But suppose you're wrong? Suppose someone could show you that you aren't on your own after all?"

She looks me over again. "If only." She sighs, then squints as she glances at the gold watch.

She will make a good New Joiner. Easy. Some Outsiders put up a fierce resistance—occasionally Howard even has to Eject them—but girls like her eat as though they've been starved once you've got them to taste the Truth.

Taste the Truth.

Howard's words.

Howard. Howard. *Eeenjant cany neary. Eeenjant cany neary.*

I pull The Book from my shoulder bag and hand it to her. "Would you look at this? It'll just take another minute."

She narrows her eyes as she reads the cover: *Why Are We Here?*

31

She sighs again. "Good question. I don't know why I'm here. I'm supposed to be at work."

"For a small donation—say about five pounds—I can let you keep it. Have a look at it tonight when you've got some spare time. It just . . . with some people it makes a difference."

"I really don't . . ."

"The donation goes to charity. Help the Blind is this week's cause. So even if you throw it in the bin later, you'll still have done something worthwhile."

She frowns, turning pages. "My eyesight's not good. It's a worry. My mother went blind suddenly at twenty-five." Her voice is changed. Wavering.

I touch her arm very lightly and she sways towards me, almost as if she is going to lean on me, then she snaps open the clip on her bronze-brown handbag, handing me a ten pound note. "I'm sorry. I don't have any change."

I glance round at Woolworth's. "I could go in and . . ."

"No. Go on. Keep it."

"Thank you. Thank you. You've done some good today."

She fluffs up her fringe with her fingers. "Try telling that to my boss when I turn up half an hour late."

"And if you ever want more information, we have regular New Joiner mornings. The venues are listed in the back of The Book." I beam her my Spread-the-Word smile again.

She hesitates, then smiles back before turning away, weaving through the streams of Outsiders, hurrying back to the life that keeps her blocked from feeling anything that matters.

I hope she comes to a New Joiner morning. I hope she will be Saved.

I am tired suddenly, but I must keep working. I have only sold three copies of The Book and I have been out since dawn. Across the cobbled square the church clock shows 2:30 P.M. Only another four and a half hours to go before the van returns. I need to try harder.

"Do you have a minute . . . ?"

"Do you have a minute . . . ?"

"Do you have a minute . . . ?"

I am still trying. Getting cold. My ankles ache, but pain is good for me. There will be worse things before Endtime is over. Howard needs to make sure we are strong enough.

The smell wafting out of a nearby restaurant makes me cross the road to avoid it. I never buy food.

The buying of food would eat into my profit. And anyway, I do not need it. When I get back, the Followers will have prepared hot bread and vegetable stew, and they will hand it round in steaming clay bowls during the late night Talk and Support session.

A narrow alley leads into a small park where a woman is pushing a little girl on a swing. Twin babies are screaming purple in their double buggy. I do not deal much with babies or children. New Joiners have them, of course, but committed Followers rarely reproduce. It is discouraged. Howard does not want the very young to suffer Endtime.

Howard. Howard.

I must sell more copies of The Book. I am wasting time.

I walk past the purple-faced twins and stop by the swing. "Your little girl is beautiful. What's her name?"

"Alice." The woman slows the swing, her arms stretching to lift the child from the seat.

"Oh no, Mummy. I want more pushing. More pushing."

I smile at the woman. "Let me push her for you, while you sort out those other two."

She hesitates.

"Please, Mummy. Please." Alice twines her arms

around the ropes and fixes her mouth in a stubborn line.

The buggy rocks.

"I don't know how you cope." I shake my head, my eyes very earnest. "It must be a real struggle when they're all demanding a bit of you at the same time."

"It can be hard work. I do love them but . . ." Suddenly she beams a smile back at me. "My name's Della. What's yours?"

"Elinor."

She is still smiling as she steps back from Alice, letting me into her space so that I can take over. This is what Role Play Training calls a Positive Outsider Response. An Outsider opening up straightaway. It hardly ever happens. Most live locked in protective shells that we have to crack our way through. Pushing the swing gently, I turn to where Della is fumbling in a wide canvas bag. "I can see that you love them. It shines out of you. But it still must be difficult."

She brings out two juice-filled bottles and shakes them. "It is at the moment. My husband works away because he can't get a job round here, and the twins are teething." She crouches beside the buggy and gives the babies their juice.

Her earrings are not real gold, but she will be a good worker. All that energy that would have gone to her children will go on True Cause. Every Outsider has something to bring, and we must save as many as we can. Although it is best not to try so hard with drunks or the homeless, or anyone whose minds are unsound. They are not usually ready for us, and we must use our time on those who are.

"But have you ever thought . . ."—I pull the swing a long way back and give Alice a launch that gets her squealing and wriggling—". . . what would happen if anything bad came along?"

"I don't get you."

"This world . . ." I shake my head again. "It seems scary sometimes, doesn't it—especially when you have children to protect. There's so much danger and corruption. Chemical damage to the planet. The threat of war . . ."

Shadows cross Della's face as she bends to stroke the cheek of the nearest twin. "You're right. But I try not to think about it. You've got to stay on the sunny side, haven't you? You'd end up in a dreadful depression if you brooded on everything you read in the papers."

"I agree. Sometimes putting on a brave face feels like the only way. But it's false, don't you think? We're denying what's really going on."

"But what else can you do? People like me can't change the world. We don't have any choice."

"You do, you know." My voice is singsong and soothing. "There is a path to a better way. A better world."

She takes the emptied bottles from the gurgling twins. "Bet that path's still thick with nettles when you get round the corner." She is trying to resist but I can hear the uncertainty at the edge of her voice.

"Look," I say, "I've got a book here. Just . . . read it. See what you think. If you decide it's rubbish you can give it to Alice to cut paper dolls out of."

Della pushes the buggy over and takes it from me. "Is it free?"

"Just five pounds. All the money goes to charity. Homeless families!" I let the swing ride on its own while Alice squeals happily.

"Hold tight, won't you, darling." Della skims the pages, then looks up at me. "Oh, why not." She fishes in her pocket and finds me a handful of change. "My husband would go nuts if he knew I was reading stuff like this but . . . well . . . he is away—and we didn't give to any charity last Christmas because money was so tight."

I smile. I am happy. The Book might get her to come to a New Joiner morning. The morning might get her to one of our Meetings. If she comes to more than one Meeting she will probably stay. If she stays, she will be saved.

"More pushing," says Alice.

I swing her high again, but by now my arms are aching. One of the twins is grizzling again.

The day has grown dusky, it is starting to drizzle, and I still have too many books in my bag. "I wish I could stay with you for longer, but I need to go." I feel a lot of warmth for Della and I hope she will come to us, but I must not press her any further. Pressing Outsiders makes them panic. "Be happy."

"You too. And thanks."

The grizzles turn to screams as I walk away, the harsh squall growing fainter as I hurry across the park and out through the gate.

The streetlamps light up specks of rain. I should go back towards the shops and see if I can catch the Outsiders who are heading home. I will not get the chance to save anyone else down here.

I am about to cross the road when I see a bald-headed man, leaning in through the passenger door of a Porsche convertible, rummaging around for something on the front seat.

We are as well-trained in car types as we are in watches and jewellery.

"Do you have a minute . . . ?"

He looks me over, then turns away to rummage again, banging the bald head on the doorframe. "Oh shit."

He is well dressed. Expensive suit. Expensive aftershave. Men like him are amongst the hardest. He has had too much for too long. But Howard has many examples of how those who resist most fiercely give most freely once they have tasted the Truth. And if he was saved, this Outsider would gain so much by gifting us all he owned. There would be so many material things he would be delivered from.

I may not have sold many books, but maybe I can make up for all my losses with him. I must try my best. Try try try.

". . . But I wonder if you ever think of what life means. What it's really about."

"Frequently." He straightens and faces me. He is small—shorter than me.

"And do you ever come up with any answers? Answers that make a difference to the way you think and feel?"

"You're interested in the way I feel?"

I give him my Spread-the-Word smile. "I'm interested in lots of things about you."

"Is that so?" He stares at me. Stares for so long I look away. The rain falls harder, drumming a beat on the soft-top roof. There is something about this man that is making me uneasy, but I must keep trying. Try try try.

"I can see you've been successful with your life. I'm sure you've worked hard—harder than most people will know or understand. But have you ever had that feeling that it isn't enough . . . that you're missing something?"

"Most definitely." His eyes seem to roam the length of my body.

I fish The Book from my bag. At least he will look at that and not me.

"I think you should read this. Take it away with you. See if anything in it makes sense."

"You're very brave, aren't you, out here in the dark all on your own?" He moves very close, but he does not look at The Book. Not even a glance. I can see in the lamplight that *Why Are We Here?* is getting soggy with rain. Would an Outsider with a Porsche give up money for a soggy book?

"It's . . . it's just a guide, really. A starting-off point."

"I like the idea of you starting me off." He takes my hand. His skin feels moist and clammy. As he pulls me closer he drops *Why Are We Here?* down into the gutter. I shiver.

"You're cold, aren't you? I'll give you a lift . . ."

I twist my hand sideways but I cannot loosen his grip. "No. I—my friends are picking me up. They'll be here soon."

"You could at least shelter with me in the car. We'd keep each other company."

"I really . . ."

And suddenly he has me by the elbow and is wrenching me forward. I pull backwards, struggling against him. I think I should bite or kick but I have never learnt violence. It is not the True Cause way. I try to shout, although I am not used to shouting either, and the sound comes out too thin and small. This is happening so fast. So fast.

And suddenly footsteps thud towards us and a voice calls, "Hey—what's up? What's going on?"

It must be Howard come to rescue me.

Howard who Saves.

And I think he will be angry because it was stupid to walk away from the town. Stupid. Stupid.

Only it is not Howard—although it is not a stranger either. Not completely. I have stared into these moss-green eyes before.

41

5

He pulls out a mobile telephone. I shrink back from it. Mobile telephones are Bad Things. All telephones are Forbidden. I should not be this close to one. Its toxic vibrations may crawl into my brain.

"I'm getting the police. Perverts like you should be locked up."

"I thought she was on the game. She came right over to me and started going on about how interesting I was. What the hell would any bloke think?"

I am trying not to cry. Stupid. Stupid. I have been so stupid. "I don't want the police. It was a misunderstanding."

The man winks, as if we share an ugly secret.

I shudder and my stomach twists, but the police

must not come. Howard would be so disappointed in me. The police would love an excuse to come snooping round. I Image for a moment Howard's face, and I feel a burn of confusion. The face looking out at me is like a stranger. An Unknown. I do not want this unknown Howard in my head. It is a Bad Thought. Howard is Our Master. Howard who Saves. I want to chant his name, to get lost in it, but I realize suddenly that I am being spoken to.

"You can't just let it drop." The moss-green eyes are angry as he turns to me. "If he doesn't get you, he'll get someone else."

"That's not the way it is." The bald man is going round to the driver's side of his Porsche. "I've got a daughter. Grown up. Two kiddies of her own. Like I said earlier, this girl was making me an offer. I get it all the time . . ." He taps his keys against the roof of the Porsche. "I don't even disrespect her for it. I mean, we've all got to make a living . . ."

"Oh, get lost then. But I've got your registration number. If ever I hear of any other girl getting grief from some greasy turd in a wankmobile like this, I'll get it splashed on the front page of every newspaper. I've got contacts. I mean it."

The man gives me one last long look, gets in his Porsche, and roars off.

The moss-green eyes are searching my face. "Are you okay?" He has his hand on my arm.

I do not know what to do. What to think. Outsiders can be dangerous and devious. Trust leads to tragedy. "I have to go."

"You're joking. D'you reckon I'm just going to let you wander off after what you've been through? Let me take you for a drink. There's a pub just the other side of the park."

"I don't drink." I will walk back to the town centre. Just wait for the van. True Cause is the true cause. True Cause is the true cause.

"Well, just come and warm up for ten minutes then. You still look pretty cut up." He is close. So close. "And I'm feeling knocked away too. I'm pretty feeble really—I don't know what I'd have done if that pervert had gone for me. I could do with a pint of something. My name's Jamie, by the way."

"I'm Elinor."

He looks at me for a long moment, and there is a sadness in the look that I cannot place. Then he nods, as if he has answered some private question in his mind. "Come on then, Elinor. Let's at least get out of this rain. We're already like a couple of drowned rats."

44

. . . A great grey rat lying lifeless in the gutter. And I could only shake my head and mutter . . . Why is it that all mankind can only seem to seek but never find?

Ten minutes. It is not long. Just a flicker of time. Ten minutes cannot cause me any harm.

6

I hate the smell of this Drinking Den. I feel as if it is soaking into my skin and my hair and when I leave the smell will still be on me and the others will know where I have been. Although Drinking Dens are not Forbidden—sometimes we can sell books or even find a New Joiner in one, but not often. More usually we are laughed at or sworn at, and we generally avoid them unless we are very desperate.

Jamie is Forbidden though. Being in a Drinking Den with Jamie is a Bad Bad Thing. What am I doing? What am I risking?

"What shall I get you?" Jamie has his hand on my back as if he thinks I may run if he loosens his hold on me. He is probably right.

"Just water. Please."

We stand at the counter and Jamie orders water and a beer.

The beer is dark and clouded. I think that the frothing must be due to something toxic and chemical, and I can understand why Outsiders often stagger when they have been drinking it.

The Outsider who serves the drinks has a red nose and red veined cheeks and eyes that stream and stream, yet he is staring at me as though I am the one who is the odd sight.

A group of young men at the other end of the counter are laughing loudly. I do not look at them, although I am fairly certain it will be me—or at least my clothes—that they find so funny.

"Let's grab a table." Jamie leads us into a corner that is shadowed and out of the way. I feel more comfortable here—or rather I would, apart from the television. It is huge, mounted on the wall, and I try to sit sideways so that I block it away, but it keeps flashing out images and I think that it may be able to corrode my thoughts even without me looking directly at it.

"You're still shivering." Jamie is opposite me. "Maybe I should get you a coffee or something as well?"

"I don't drink coffee."

"Coffee's banned?"

I nod, rubbing my hands to ease the cold out of them, and then thinking that it is not fair that I am getting comfortable while the others are still out selling books in the rain. "Coffee is a toxin."

"Well—cheers." He raises his glass in a strange Outsider drinking gesture, then sips his beer. The froth whitens his upper lip. I think that he looks different without the mud smears and his hair all tangled. But he still draws me. I cannot understand why. "What else is banned?" I realize he is smiling at me.

I struggle to give an answer that is bland. "It's not that things are so much Forbidden," I say in the end. "It's just that we don't have them. It's for our own good. We wouldn't want to drink coffee."

"Fair enough." He is watching me closely. "So—do you eat good stuff? Healthy stuff, I mean."

"Rice mainly. Fruit and vegetables. Sometimes bread . . ." I stop. I am telling him too much. We always let New Joiners *discover* how we live. We never just tell them. "Maybe you should read this . . ."

I pull The Book from my bag and he takes it, glances at the cover, then lets it drop on the table. He is still watching me, as if there might be secrets written across my face. "Do you really really believe it? Deep down inside?"

I trace my finger round the rim of my glass. I usually have answers for Outsiders—quick-fire answers that can shoot down anything they say. But not today. Today I am struggling. Howard Our Master. Howard who Saves. Why can I not Image him the way I usually do? The television is flickering and I am still terrified that it is invading my thoughts. Television is a form of Mind Control. It drains the brain cells of Outsiders so they cannot think for themselves anymore.

"Is it true you don't have electricity?"

"We have gas. Everything gas."

"But electricity is safer—and easier."

"Howard says electricity is an evil." For a moment I am not certain why Howard feels this, but the doubt scares me, and I do not let it grow in my mind.

"That's insane. How could the world have got to where it is without electricity?"

"The place the world is at present is not a good one." My Role Play answers are flashing back to me now. "True Cause teaches us to walk with nature rather than run with technology. An easy life breeds carelessness. Carelessness is foolishness . . ."

"But your Howard—he lords it up in that

mansion, and drives round in a stretch limo. That's a pretty easy life, isn't it?"

"Howard has to conserve his energy because he is weighted with the greatest of burdens."

"What if I said you were just brainwashed into thinking that?"

"All Outsiders think that. It's just because they don't understand."

"Help me see it your way, then."

I have moved on to safer ground. This is a well-trodden argument and I relax. I am in control again. I will not let True Cause down. "Well—here's one thing. Why do you think it's so wrong for Howard to live well? Lots of Outsiders yearn for riches. Lots of your major companies have managers who live in splendour, while their workers struggle to get by. Howard has a greater purpose. The Highest Calling. Those manager types are only pleasing themselves."

"Elinor—Elinor . . ." Jamie leans forward in his seat, shaking his head. "I don't want to believe you buy all of this without asking questions."

I look back at him. "We are happy." I am suddenly desperate to make him see my side. "So happy. How many Outsiders are really happy? The suicide rate last year rose to nearly 7,000 people. No Follower has ever taken their own life. No Follower would want to. When New Joiners come to us they learn how to be properly loved. How to be part of a cause that is working towards something that matters. And when Endtime comes we will be saved, and be part of the New Beginning. How can wanting that be wrong? And how can your Outsider world compete?"

"Shit." He leans back again. "I can't concentrate when you look at me like that. Your eyes and your hair and everything. You're—you're so beautiful."

Beautiful. Beautiful. I should quick-fire back at him again. The outer form is nothing and nowhere. We learn to love the soul within. We learn to love the soul within. But I say nothing. He called me beautiful. He called me beautiful. In my confusion I turn my head and see a woman on the television. I let myself look at her. Stare at her. Is she beautiful? How do Outsiders decide these things?

I realize the screen of the television is made up of dots. Tiny fuzzed splotches. Hundreds of them. And a fuzzed idea uncurls in me that, if I stop thinking for True Cause, who will I begin to think for?

Suddenly panic pulls at me. These are Bad Thoughts. Maybe my brain cells are already being drained. A slow trickle of whatever I have been is seeping out of them. I turn back to look at Jamie.

He is still looking at me.

His hair has curled as it dried. In the dingy light of the Drinking Den his eyes are a darker green. But still that warmth. That warmth.

"Meet me again," he says suddenly.

He takes my hand. Just holds it. I can feel the heat burn through his skin and into mine. "I can't do this," I whisper. "I mustn't. I really mustn't."

But he just keeps holding my hand, and I do not take it away.

7

"Look into my eyes. Relax and unwind. Let your thoughts flow out of you."

The Counsellor is new. A lot of the Prediction Practice Counsellors are. They have received special training and only those who are of an exceptionally High Order are allowed to work with us. It is vital that we develop good Prediction Practice skills so that we can be properly prepared.

Howard says that a bad Prediction Practice session could cause us years of damage, and he is not taking any risks.

Howard is so careful. So caring.

And I am the one who has been taking risks. Risking my future, and his pain.

Meet me again. Meet me again.

I need to wire up a fence inside my head, to keep Jamie out.

The Counsellor must not see him walking through my thoughts.

I force myself to stare into the Counsellor's eyes. They are a watered grey, his face haloed by gaslight that washes down from the stable wall.

Meet me again. Meet me again.

"What are you thinking?" The Counsellor's voice is level and low. His water-grey eyes never leave my face.

"I . . . I'm not sure."

"Put all your trust in me, and Image something special in your mind. Don't try and force it. What comes will come."

I notice that his water-grey eyes hold pins of light that burn like fever in the centre. I shift in my seat, suddenly uncomfortable.

"What makes you happy?"

"Being part of True Cause. Part of Howard's vision." I make my voice as level and low as his, and Image my fence.

"Can you see Howard's vision? Can you let it move through you?"

I have been coming to Prediction Practice for

several years now, and nothing has ever moved through me. It has for the other Chosen. They come back exhausted, talking about Sudden Sight and Flashes of the Future and all the terrors and the glories to come.

"I . . . I'm not sure."

"Can you see anything at all?"

"A fence. Very high." At least I can be honest about this.

"A fence." The Counsellor nods, the pinprick in his eyes sparking new light.

Meet me again. Meet me again.

"The fence in your head is shielding something dangerous, isn't it? Something you're scared of showing me?"

"Yes." I realize I am drifting on his voice. I am letting him in.

"We need to cut the fence away. I'll be with you. There's nothing to be scared of. Image your fence now. What is it made of?"

"Fine mesh. With barbs along the top." My voice is a long way off.

"Close your eyes. Keep them shut. I want to reassure you that this fence will not hurt you. The barbs will be soft if you touch them. Can you tell me that now? Tell me what you know about the fence."

"It will not hurt me. It will not hurt me."

"And now, in your mind, take some pliers and cut a tiny hole in that mesh. Make it just big enough to see through."

I cut the wire.

Memories scratch at me. I said goodbye in the Drinking Den, refusing to let him walk with me. On the journey back the van rattled from a loose exhaust, and everyone joined hands and sang. I was separate. Watching them as if I had never watched them before. And remembering Jamie. I knew he was a Bad Thought, but the memory had a sweetness to it. Sweet as a stolen strawberry.

In my Image I suddenly see strawberries. A whole field of them. True Cause strawberries. And me and Meryl picking them for the market and once—just once—I stole one and ate it.

"What can you see now, Elinor?"

"Strawberries."

That strawberry stained my lips. Meryl made me rub the stain away before anyone saw. I paid for it later though. I got a rash across my belly, and I knew it was because I had done a Bad Thing. But I have never since tasted a strawberry so sweet.

"And what do strawberries mean to you, Elinor?"

Meet me again. Meet me again.

"Sweet—and dangerous." He must know. He must see. Only the very skilled can work with us.

"So behind your fence you see sweetness and danger?"

Jamie's eyes. Jamie's voice. A small punnet of time can be filled with so much.

"It's clear to me what you're seeing, Elinor. I'm seeing it too, now. We are there together."

So this is it. The Truth will be squashed out of me. There is relief in this knowledge. It is the path back to safety. True Cause. True Cause.

"You're tapping into Endtime, Elinor. Red for danger. Red for strawberries. The blood of destruction, and the pure untainted fruit that will burst out beyond the devastation. That's what you're seeing, isn't it? Isn't it?"

This must be a test. I shake my head, my hands pressing against my temples. "It's not just the strawberries. That's . . . that's not all I can see . . ."

"No. No. Not all. Of course not all. Can you see the tormented trees bend and break? The rage of gold that spits and burns?"

"I can't . . ."

"You can, Elinor. You can. When the time comes you will be ready for this. And when the terror is done you will rise up, as all True Cause Followers will, and Howard will come for us and we will go forward together into the New Beginning. That's what you see, isn't it, Elinor? That's what you see?"

I suddenly feel I have woken from a dream and I am watching the Counsellor. He is feasting on his own words, his eyes pressed shut.

How has this happened?

The water-grey eyes blink open again. They burn with joy. He smiles. "You have experienced Sudden Sight, and a Flash of the Future," he tells me. "We reached behind your fence. We saw Endtime together."

He hugs me, then holds me back at arm's length. "Some of the data from your previous sessions was disturbing; but today, when I write up these notes for Howard, he will be elated. With both of us."

I Image Howard reading these notes. Will he really be Elated, like the Counsellor is? Or will he see the truth? The Counsellor is still holding my hands. He is shining like the sun, beaming light and warmth. I am suddenly cold.

Meet me again. Meet me again.

8

I look across to where Isabel is trimming the edges of a poster.

A NEW BEGINNING

Tired? Sick? Lonely? Depressed?

Or just questioning the emptiness of life.
The daily futility.

THERE ARE ANSWERS.
THERE IS A REASON.

Come and share warmth with us.
We will give hope and purpose to your life.
We love you.

Weekly gathering at . . . .

Isabel's blonde hair is touched by a line of light that points in through the narrow School Room window, and I think about how Howard tells us he can see light glowing out of us, different colours for different moods.

I do not think that the colour that glows out of me can be very bright at the moment. I will have to stand near the back at the next meeting, in the hope that he will not see.

"We need to collect those snowdrops for the New Joiner blessings," I tell Isabel suddenly. "I think we should go now."

My voice trembles—perhaps guilt unsteadies it—although the need for the snowdrops is true. Once a month we bring in seasonal leaves and flowers to decorate Star Temple for the Ceremony of Faith, when New Joiners become sealed as True Cause Followers.

"All those lost Outsiders saved." Isabel rolls up the poster and comes to help me unstack two baskets from the corner of the School Room. "I wish I could bring in more. There are so many we will never reach."

"So many," I agree. But as she links arms with me and we head out through the yard I am not thinking about saving anyone. Instead I am thinking of the way my face is shaped. The way my body moves as I walk. What exactly is it about my eyes?

He called me beautiful.

It plagues me, the idea of being beautiful. I want it, and I want to push it away. "Have you ever thought about how you look?" I say to Isabel.

"Never!" Isabel's voice is grave. "The outer form is nothing and nowhere. We learn to love the soul within."

"We learn to love the soul within," I murmur. I do not say anything else, but I am thinking that we look alike, Isabel and me. In fact, all of us Chosen are the same sort of build. And fair. That is another thing. We are all fair. Why have I never noticed this before?

Part of me wants these Bad Thoughts to stop. I want to slot back into the safety of True Cause thinking. I do not want all these strange ideas that pull and twist and tie knots in my head.

But there is another part—something stirring in me—like a stranger who is stepping out from the dark at the back of my mind—a stranger who is hungry to reach the woods. And she is not looking for snowdrops.

I am sure he will be beside that same tree, just waiting.

I have shrunk from this. And longed for it.

How has he done this to me? Outsiders can be dangerous and devious. Trust leads to tragedy.

But I still keep walking.

We enter the wood and take the holly trail—the way I did that first day. Our boots squelch and sink with every step. It is hard work, and several times Isabel slips, nearly bringing us both down. "Why are we going this way? It's much easier further along."

"Meryl and I found great clumps of snowdrops when we went this way last year. Trust me."

Trust me.

Trust me.

What am I becoming?

She trusts me, falling behind where the trail gets too narrow. "The holly's so dense," she calls out. "I keep getting my skirt snagged."

I notice that I am glad she is no longer holding my hand. My hand is free. I can swing it. Stretch it. I do neither of these things, but it excites me to think that I could.

He called me beautiful.

"Elinor. Please. Slow down."

"Sorry." I am sorry. Isabel is my Shadow. I should be taking care of her. I wait for her, then walk more slowly.

We are so near the tree now, near to where we met—and my heart feels suddenly squeezed.

But he is not anywhere obvious, and I have a sudden panic that he may surprise me at any time, the way he did before. I have been stupid again. Stupid stupid. Suppose he rushes over to greet me as if we are two Outsiders in a street. Isabel will know that something has already passed between us and she will have to Unburden when we get back. She will have no choice.

These things press in my head. I should not have come. Outsiders can be dangerous and devious. Trust leads to tragedy.

"I still can't see any snowdrops." Isabel comes up beside me. The path has widened into the clearing and she takes my hand again as she goes on. "Maybe we should listen for them. Howard is always hearing flowers sing. If we let ourselves tune in properly, we might hear them too."

We stand pressed close in the shadowed silence—Isabel now listening for the songs of snowdrops, and me listening for . . . for what? Twigs breaking? A scrunch of leaves? I will hear him soon.

But I hear nothing, and the knowledge seeps in slowly that he is not here. I had not expected this emptiness.

What did I want? I cannot answer my own question, but I am facing my whole life and Endtime and eternity without seeing him again. And it hurts.

"Oh, look . . . !" Isabel gives a breathless squeal. My knees become liquid and I have to lean against the tree to stay steady. She must have seen him.

I swallow and breathe deeply, my eyes following to where she is pointing. Just beyond the thinning straggle of holly, and before the next line of trees, there is . . . a clump of snowdrops growing. No Jamie at all.

I have been being pathetic.

I feel shamed suddenly by all the things I have been thinking and hoping. I will block him away. He was a kind of a dream. Or maybe a test. True Cause is the true cause. True cause is the true cause. I will never let him bring me Bad Thoughts again.

9

Outsiders are clustering around us, even though we are only just setting up our stall. There is still plenty of stock to unload from the back of the van. But Outsiders are like that. Always grabbing at bargains.

"How much for this?" A woman is picking up a green floral plate and turning it upside down to see where it was made. Where things are made is important to Outsiders. For lots of them it does not seem to matter whether they actually like something or not—just what it is worth.

"Twenty pounds," I say. "It's brand new. Unwanted present."

The woman holds the plate higher and squints at it. She is hoping for a chip or a crack that will help her to get the price down. She will not find one. We would never sell rubbish—everything is checked out and in good condition—it is all the clearings from New Joiners' houses. Once they come to us they do not need all their clutter anymore.

"I'll give you ten," says the woman, still clutching the china. In her mind it is already hers. She will not be able to let it go.

"Will you take fifteen for that?" A man who has been hovering behind her pushes closer, and touches the rim of the plate.

The woman glares at him and edges slightly out of his reach.

"Well—I wanted twenty . . ." I smile at the man and pretend to hesitate.

The woman thrusts a twenty pound note at me—it has been in her hand all the time.

"Go on," she says quickly. "I'm probably a fool but I'll give you what you're asking." I take it from her and push it into my money bag.

The man gives me a brief nod, and merges back into the crowd. I know him, of course. One of the Watchers. They are here to help us get the best prices, and they cruise round all our stalls pretending to be Outsiders but really checking to see that everything is going all right.

Isabel climbs out from the back of the van and hands me a bundle of scarves. "There's still lots of clothes to come out. I'll put the rack up."

I would help her, but suddenly I get very busy.

"Excuse me—how much for this bag?"

"Will you take a fiver for this CD?"

"This elephant—is it actually ivory?"

I think about all these Outsiders moving round their homes, picking their way between all these "things." Howard says possessions weigh down the soul. Our sheds are very basic. The walls have been whitewashed to make up for the lack of windows, and one gas lamp, which hangs at the far end, is lit every night. Each shed has bunks for us to sleep in, and a blanket box. Our dresses are hung on racks at one end, and there are built-in cupboards with towels and toiletries. We do not need anything else, and anyway what would be the point? "Things" will not survive beyond Endtime.

The field is filling up with stalls. Opposite us a hot dog van has arrived.

Howard has a fleet of hot dog vans. I have worked in them sometimes, although I have never eaten a hot dog. We are all vegetarians, of course. Howard says that the eating of another creature's flesh is amongst the vilest of Outsider behaviours.

Our hot dog vans bring in good money though. Much much more than The Book ever does.

"Do you want some water?" Isabel comes up behind me. She has a bottle and pours some into a clay cup. It is cold, and the ice bites my throat, but I am grateful for it. It is still early morning, but we had our fruit and rice before dawn, and the smell of the onions opposite is bringing in Bad Thoughts.

There is a squeal and a laugh from beside the hot dog van, and I look up to see a group of Outsiders—my sort of age—laughing and shoving at each other.

"Get off me, Nathan." A girl in a studded blue jacket and tight jeans jumps backwards as a boy grabs the tomato ketchup from the counter and squirts her with it. "That's really gross."

Still giggling, she ducks behind another boy, putting her arms round his waist. "Save me, Jamie. Save me."

I freeze. I am colder than ice water.

Jamie.

I watch him slip his arm round her shoulder and it is as if someone is scratching ice across my heart.

"Leave off her, Nathan." Jamie is laughing. They are all laughing. Jamie has a hot dog, and he passes it to the stud jacket girl. She bites it, wipes her mouth with the back of her hand, then hands it back. He takes another bite, then holds it for her again.

I want to get away, but I am caged by clutter and clothes racks and the van behind me. A bite for him. A bite for her. A bite for him. A bite for her. And then he is wiping her fingers on a white napkin and she is smiling and his other arm is still round her shoulders.

He looks up. Over at me.

I think, for a sickened moment, that he will walk away, but his arm drops from her and he comes over—springs over—his face alive in a way I have never seen on anyone ever.

"It's you," he says.

I stare down at the stall, suddenly needing to rearrange the scarves. "It's me," I say.

"I wanted to find you. I just didn't know how to start."

I know I should pretend not to understand but his closeness is dizzying.

Stud jacket comes over and begins riffling through some beaded bracelets, wrinkling her nose as if we might have threaded them with deer droppings. She picks up a bracelet and dangles it in front of me. "Bit naff, aren't they?"

I am not sure what naff means, but I can tell it is not anything good. "It's all for charity. Third world poverty."

Stud jacket lights a cigarette. "I'm sure it is."

"Leave it, Naomi." Jamie hasn't taken his eyes off me.

I am looking everywhere but back at him.

"Sorreeeeeeeee." Naomi shrugs and wanders away. She still has the naff bracelet.

"I'll pay for what she took," Jamie says. "How much?"

His voice. His voice.

"Two pounds."

He glances behind me, and then says softly, "I wish we could meet up. Talk again and stuff."

My hand is shaking.

My heart is shaking.

I do not know how to answer, so I say nothing.

"How about the woods? If I went there again, about this time tomorrow morning, would you come?"

There is a knot in one of the scarves. I pick and pick at it. I am going to say "no." I have to say "no." Then, for the first time, I meet his look. "Yes," I say softly. "I'll come."

10

I will not go. Of course I will not go. I lie on my bunk staring up at the beamed ceiling, watching the cobwebs in the light of the gas lamp. Even if I wanted to go, I would not be able to get there. It would be impossible to get away.

Below me Isabel shifts and mutters. Apart from a few rustlings and grunts, everyone is sleeping heavily.

Where is he now? What is he doing?

I pull my blanket up over my head and huddle in deeper, curling so that my arms lock around my knees. My thoughts are like roots that wind tighter and tighter. I want to prune them out, leave space in my head and concentrate on the things that really matter.

True Cause is the true cause. True Cause is the true cause.

He is probably asleep. I grow an Image of him, sprawled in his Outsider bed. In the image his skin is paled by moonlight. I trace the shapes of his face with my memory. It is just a face. Why this face and not a thousand others? Why am I letting him matter?

The night stretches. An owl hoots. The cock crows.

. . . And then the wake-up bell rings, shrill and fierce, and the Morning Message crackles out from the yard. *"Another day has been gifted to us. Another day to prepare. Trust in True Cause. We are on the path to paradise."*

Felicity and Imogen stumble past, their towels under their arms.

"Happy morning, you sleepy heads, we love you," they say.

"Happy morning. Love you too." Isabel moves from her bunk and stretches up to tug at my blanket. "Come on, Elinor. The bell's gone."

She pulls the blanket from me and I know that if only she had left me alone I could have slept for days. Years. For all of eternity.

"All right. Don't do that. I'm just coming."

She nudges me again and I have to stop myself

from shouting at her. I must not shout. We never shout. I climb down from my bunk and hug her. She leans into me and the anger prickles me again, like a rash. It takes everything I have not to push her away.

"I'm going to the cleansing-cubicles," I say quickly. "I won't be long."

I am long though. The icy water that usually batters me awake just makes me numb. I tilt my head up, letting it pour into my eyes and my mouth and I stand like that for a long time, shivering and staring at the wall.

"Elinor—are you all right?" Isabel taps on the door.

"Coming." I turn the water off but still stand for another minute.

Is he awake yet? Is he thinking about me?

"Elinor?"

"Sorry—yes—I'm on my way." I pull my towel around me. I will not keep doing this. I will not let him run like a demon round my head.

As I walk back to join Isabel in our room I see she has straightened my bunk and I smile at her. "Thank you."

"You seem tired. I wanted to help you."

"That's kind. Thank you." It is kind. I am lucky. So lucky.

"I love you."

"I love you."

I take the rust-brown Monday dress down from the rack, and Isabel comes across to zip me up. The dress is shapeless and loose. I remember how Naomi had curves and bumps even in the studded jacket. I pull the dress in at the sides so that it follows the line of my waist. "Do I look very thin?"

"The outer form is nothing and nowhere. We learn to love the soul within."

"We learn to love the soul within," I reply.

It begins to rain outside, a heavy shower that smacks down onto the tin roof. I think of him standing in the woods. The rain will curl his hair again. How long will he wait?

Snatching up my comb I start attacking the knots in my hair. It hurts, and I am glad.

"Here. Let me do that for you." Isabel takes the comb and begins working with soft, gentle strokes. I close my eyes, and his face is there again.

And suddenly I know that I cannot do it. Cannot leave him standing there. I will find a way to go— just this one time—to tell him it is hopeless.

Just to do that is not such a Bad Thing. Because then it will all be over and I can get back to my world, and he can get back to his. I feel a wrench as

I think this, as if something is being torn from me, and turn sharply to Isabel. "What do you think of the name Naomi?"

"It's nice."

"I hate it." I say this unexpectedly. I had not known I was thinking it. Now I let the idea of hate jab me like something hard and spiked. I have never hated anything before. It has never even occurred to me that I could.

Grabbing the comb back from Isabel I begin tearing at the tangles again.

11

What must be, must be. Everything is for a reason.

The Monday message stretches on its banner across the entrance to the dining marquee. I stare at it for a moment, and although I have read it once a week for most of my life, it is as if I am seeing it for the first time. "What do you think that actually means?" I say to Isabel.

Isabel brushes the rain from her eyes and we shuffle forward in the breakfast line. "We are all part of Howard's Great Plan. We do not need to question anything."

I want to shake her suddenly—that flatness to her voice. What I am asking is important. I need to make her *think* about it. Because if everything happens for a reason then maybe my meeting Jamie is part of Howard's Great Plan. Maybe I am allowed to go.

"So if something happened, something that seemed like a Bad Thing, how could you tell that it wasn't really a Bad Thing but a thing that had been sent to help you learn something."

She looks away, uncomfortable. "Those questions are for Unburdenings, aren't they? We must trust True Cause."

"We must trust True Cause," I repeat hurriedly.

The line moves forward, and we edge out of the rain and inside. The marquee smells of toast and boiled rice, and watching the Followers ahead of me take their clay bowls and mugs of lemon water to the benches my stomach groans. "Only ten Followers before us," I say to Isabel. "We won't be long."

"There's no fruit on the end table." Her voice is puzzled as she strains forward, craning her neck. "Monday is normally a fruit day."

"Must be another of Howard's messages from the Divine Writings," I say. "It must have told him to change the order of things again." I have a sudden urge to laugh when I say this, although this strange mood also scares me. I should not be laughing at Howard. Howard Our Master. Howard who Saves.

And anyway Isabel is not laughing. "Whatever he does, it is for the good of us all," she says.

I think suddenly that the brown Monday dress does not flatter her skin, and I wonder if it looks harsh on me too. Although there are not many choices. All our dresses are shades of brown or green, except for Sunday, when we must all wear white. White would not do well in the woods.

We are close to the food. They are sprinkling the rice with nuts and raisins, which is my favourite mix. I Image reaching forward and grabbing a handful of the mix from out of the serving tray. In the Image I eat from my hand. Cram it into my mouth. The Image rocks me and I think that I am actually going to push forward and do it. I lock my arms across my chest and whisper a True Cause chant. "Greed feeds gremlins. Gremlins eat the soul. Greed feeds gremlins. Gremlins eat the soul."

Isabel joins me, and we chant softly but urgently as I try to blot out the pains in my stomach. I am feeling giddy.

Above us the rain thrums a rhythm on the roof and the rhythm makes shapes in my mind that I try to make sense of, but as soon as I think I might have worked them out, they dance away. I can see coloured spots that hover on either side of my line of vision. We are now only three Followers away from the food.

Greed feeds gremlins. Gremlins eat the soul. Once I have eaten, the buzzing in my head will go away. My head often buzzes before breakfast.

I stare up at the mould on the inside of the canvas and notice trickles of water have found their way through where the fabric is rotting. New Joiners will be assigned to stitch patches onto it again. This marquee has been here a long time—ever since some Outsider war a few years ago when a great mass of New Joiners suddenly flocked to us and we could not fit in the barn anymore—but if Endtime is near there is little point in Howard spending precious True Cause money on replacing it.

The Followers in front get their food and edge away to the tables. They have to stand because there are not enough seats. There are never enough seats. It is our turn. I pick up a bowl, and hand one to Isabel. The Follower who is serving has skin like grey dough.

Everything in my head is food. Greed feeds gremlins. Greed feeds gremlins.

She keeps her eyes lowered as she dips the ladle into the rice, levelling it out with the edge of a knife. Rice and raisins slip back into her dish, and I think that the levelling has cost me at least two mouthfuls. It is for the good of us all. For the good of us all. Although just in this moment I cannot work out what, or why.

Suddenly the marquee loudspeaker cracks out an order. "Emergency. Emergency. All Followers to gather in Star Temple. All Followers to gather in Star Temple."

The dough-skinned Follower empties my rice back into her tray. Gremlins eat the soul. Gremlins eat the soul.

There will be no more food until this evening.

Those Followers who are halfway through eating push their plates away and leave their breakfast unfinished on the tables.

"Come on." Isabel takes the bowl that I cannot quite bear to let go of, and links her arm through mine. "We must go."

The loudspeaker rasps its command again. "Emergency. Emergency. There is little time. There is little time."

"It must be terrible for Howard to know what he knows." Isabel is steering me away from the food.

I try to keep with her but I am dizzy. So dizzy. The marquee is moving. The roof is upside down. Or maybe I am upside down.

"I can't," I say. Or I think I say. "I don't feel too good."

"Shall I call a Carer?" The marquee is empty now, the last crush of Followers disappearing out into the rain.

"I'll be all right. I'll catch up with you. Honestly."

Honestly. Honestly. The word sticks in my throat. Will lightning strike me down? Will the earth boil and split and swallow me up? Because I will not catch up with her. I will grab a handful of somebody's abandoned rice and stuff it in my mouth, and when I feel better I will make this my chance.

Everyone will be in the meeting. It is only the Watchers I need to be wary of—there will still be some patrolling the site.

Beware and be wary.

Beware and be wary.

What am I doing?

12

"You came." He has the scratched, slightly muddy look again. I wonder if he has to dig his way in to get here.

"I came."

"Is it safe for you?"

I do not answer, because I am scared that if I tell him the truth, he will go.

"Look—I won't hurt you or anything. You'll be okay with me."

"I know." I do know, although I do not know how.

It has stopped raining but the trees still drip round us. He touches my arm and leads me through a tunnel of branches which end in a twist of ivy and vines that curve to make a roof, like an upturned nest. "It's dry in here. I've already checked it out."

There is a circle of trees, and a fallen trunk, and he tears at more ivy that has wrapped round it. "Here. Have a seat."

I sit. What will I say? What will we talk about? I realize I have a leaf caught in my hair and I pull it out, shredding it with my fingers. The brittle flakes land on the skirt of my dress, although they are hard to see because the rusted brown is so similar.

He goes to a hollow in one of the trees. "Secret hiding place," he grins. "We could leave each other messages. If things get too desperate, I'll put some sort of code in here, and wait for you in the road."

I cannot catch his meaning, and my face must look blank because he shrugs, shakes his head, then says, "I stashed some stuff in here. A sort of picnic." I watch him take out two paper bags and some bottles of water. "I got the pasties from the bakery. Fresh this morning. Wholemeal."

I nod and smile, although I am nervous of sharing a whole meal with him, and I have no knowledge of what a pasty is.

I have to say something. The silence is a weight between us. "Is it hard for you? Getting in?"

He looks troubled for a moment, and I think I

have said the wrong thing, but then he shrugs again. "There's a dodgy bit in the fence—down past a stream. It's not big, but it's enough. I reckon it's better I don't tell you any more than that—you might give it away to one of your lot by accident. Then they'll block it up and I won't be able to get here at all."

I start when he says that. It is not the first part, it is the second. *I won't be able to get here at all.* It must mean he wants this to happen again. He does not see this as the only time.

"Here's your pasty."

"Thank you." The pasty scares me. It is a mound of pastry, which is probably all right, but there could be anything inside.

"I would've got pizza but they'd sold out of the cheese ones and I took a guess you'd be vegetarian."

I am still staring at the pasty. I am relieved he has told me there is no meat in it, but Outsiders put all sorts of toxins in their food. It is a big risk. Perhaps I can just nibble the edges. I had the handful of rice earlier, so the greed and the gremlins have faded.

"Right—let's go for it." He raises his own pasty in the air and shoots me a half smile. "I don't know about you but I'm famished."

I have to look away because the half smile lights his face in a way that hurts me. Famished. I have not met this word, but I think I understand it. It must come from famine. There will be great famine at Endtime. It is why Followers have to eat so much less than Outsiders, to help us be prepared.

I break off tiny edges of the pasty and test them on my lips. I do not die horribly. I do not even collapse in a spasm of food poisoning. And suddenly I take a bite—a proper bite—and my mouth tastes the filling and it is neither wonderful nor terrible and I have still not collapsed writhing in pain.

There are crumbs on my lap, mixed up with the brittle brown leaf. I stand to brush them off, and Jamie pulls a white napkin from his strap bag and hands it to me. "I've thought of everything," he says.

I am thinking of everything too. I am thinking of everything I watched when he shared the hot dog with stud jacket Naomi. He wiped sauce from her hands with a napkin like this. The pasty is suddenly a stodge in my mouth. Why does the memory stab me?

"So—tell me more about your stuff. The way you live and everything."

I try to flatten down the hardness that spikes through me again.

"We live on the farm. Well—it's been converted to accommodate as many Followers as possible. The overspill—mainly New Joiners—live in tents and vans and old buses in the back fields."

"How many of you are there?"

"I'm not sure. It's growing so fast and we . . . I don't mix with everyone." I have to be careful here. I must not explain about being Chosen. Only New Joiners who have been initiated into the Sealing Ceremony are allowed to know what being Chosen actually means. And even then they do not know everything.

There is a gap in the talking. Above and about the rooks are calling and I look up at them through the branches. I feel I should ask Jamie some questions too, but I am not sure what might matter to him. Then I remember the notebook. "You said you scribble down ideas. Do you write stories?"

He shakes his head. "Not fiction. More factual. So—where do you actually live?" He seems keen to push the focus back to me.

"It was a cowshed once. I share it with eleven—sorry, ten—other girls."

"Are you all the same age?"

"I'm the oldest. Fifteen. The youngest is Gabriella, and I think she's seven."

"Fifteen?" He squints at me, and I am not sure if he is thinking that fifteen is good or bad. Then he nods. "That sounds about right."

I wonder what it is about right for, but I do not get time to ask because he comes in with the next question.

"And school? You must have a school?"

"So many things you want to know." I smile at him although I am not completely comfortable either. I should make him come and see—not just keep laying my life out as if it is a kind of market stall for him to pick through. But he has edged slightly closer, his arm pressed against mine, and it feels comfortable. So comfortable. "We do English and Maths and Science just the same as Outsider children. Inspectors come in and check that we're covering all the main things. But we have other lessons too. Lessons that are special for us."

"Like?" He opens his bottle of water, which has a blue plastic spout, and passes the other bottle to me. I do not open mine because I am not sure how to. The spout idea is strange and I would feel awkward if he watched me fumbling with it.

I wrap the half eaten pasty up in the white napkin and balance it beside me. Even without the Naomi memory, I have had enough.

I am not sure what else I can tell him. Prediction Practice and Role Play Training and Late Night Talk and Support. None of it will mean anything. How could it? But luckily I am saved from saying anything more by a sudden shrill noise. I jump up from the trunk, thinking it is a Watcher sounding some sort of an alarm, but Jamie snatches something from his pocket. "Bugger. Sorry. I thought I'd turned it off." I am shaking all over. Taking risks. Such risks.

"It's my mobile." He frowns up at me. "I thought you were about to run for it then. You must've heard one before?"

I sit back down. "I . . . yes . . . of course." I try to push down the swell of panic. "I just try and stay away from them. They damage your brain."

He laughs then. It hits me—unsteadies me—that I have never seen anyone laugh before. Not so freely. Not so openly. "Do I look brain-damaged?"

I search his face. He doesn't. He isn't. He hands the mobile telephone to me and I hold it nervously. "Will it make that noise again?"

"I've turned the sound off. It was a crap thing, leaving it on. I'm sorry."

"How does it work?"

I know it is a Bad Thing, but I am suddenly fascinated. "How do you talk to people with it?"

"It's a bit like a talking box—a sort of radio. If you think of a city, say Claymouth, and imagine it divided down into lots of sections, and then see each section having a station which has a tower and all the radio stuff in it . . ."

I nod, although I have no idea what he is talking about.

"When someone wants to call you, their mobile zaps out a signal to the nearest station, and then that station starts sending out signals to find out where your phone is . . ."

I frown. "How does their mobile telephone know that its owner wants to contact you?"

"They tell it."

I stare at the mobile telephone, Imaging myself giving instructions to this metal box. "What do they say to it?"

Jamie laughs. "They don't say anything. Every mobile's got its own number, and each number is unique—like a code. You punch the number in, and the signal goes off to do its search."

I turn the mobile telephone over and over. Up in the trees the rooks are shouting. I am running with technology. "You mean these numbers—on the front?"

"No. They all have those. That's just the buttons. My number's 0781 781781."

0781 781781. I Image it and it glows gold, like treasure. Something of his. Something unique.

"Who knows—you might decide to call me one day." He sounds almost excited, and I am sorry that I have to let him down.

I hand it back to him. "I'm not allowed to use any sort of telephone. And even if I was, I'd never remember the number. You must have to carry loads round in your head."

"Course not. You would just punch all your mates' codes into the mobile's memory. Then, when you want to access one, you just scroll down the names. Look . . ."

He is scrolling down. The names roll past.

Martin . . . Nathan . . . Naomi.

I stop looking. Naomi. Naomi. She is everywhere. In everything. The white napkin has fallen down to the ground and I see that ants have got inside and are crawling across the pasty. "There's no point showing me any more. I wouldn't want my own telephone. There's nothing I'd need it for, and anyway telephones are Forbidden."

My voice has hardened. I feel hardened.

"What's up?" Jamie slips the mobile phone back in his pocket. "You look upset."

I shake my head. How can I tell him that Naomi

plagues me. How can I explain the way she keeps crawling through my head.

"It's nothing. Just—I've been away too long. They'll miss me."

"Sorry. Again."

I can feel him looking and looking at me. I keep staring at the pasty and the steady march of ants, and I am about to get up, to say goodbye and know that I am never coming back again, when I feel his arm slide round my shoulders. I suddenly cannot speak or even think and it is as if everything in me is melting.

"Elinor." His voice. His voice. "I don't know what to do about you. It isn't supposed to be happening like this."

I look at him, not understanding what he means, but before I can ask he tilts his head towards me and our lips touch. It is a fragment of time. Less than a second. Longer than life. I have no words to describe the rush that I feel. Except that it is beautiful.

13

I am not asleep when the bell rings, and I sit bolt upright in my bunk, fear clawing me. It is not the harsh command of the meeting bell, nor the shrill early morning wake-up call.

It is a ring we have practised many times before, but never at night and never without being told it was going to happen.

Endtime.

Isabel is halfway up my ladder, tugging the blanket, her voice shaking. "Elinor—in the emergency meeting—the one you missed because you were sick—Howard said we should be ready for a Grand Calling. This is it. Get up."

I nod. I was lucky—so lucky—this morning. No

one noticed I was missing. It has helped me to know that going to Jamie was the Right Thing. It was made easy for me.

"Elinor, Elinor." Imogen and Felicity are behind her, calling me in small thin voices.

"It's all right. I'm coming." I am the eldest and I feel it suddenly, swinging my legs down from the bunk.

Endtime. Endtime.

I have spent so much of my life waiting for this to happen, but now it is here I am not sure how to behave.

"Do we need anything?" Imogen's eyes are shocked and wide. Felicity leans against her, twisting the hem of her nightdress in her hand and whimpering like a small child.

"I—don't think so." What could we need? What could we possibly take?

The other Chosen stumble over to us. I do a quick head check, the way we have been trained. Isabel. Imogen. Felicity. Rebecca. Rachel and Laura. Elizabeth and Lucy. Sarah, stick-thin little Gabriella, and me.

We huddle together, not wanting to move. As if standing still could freeze up time. It is Isabel and not me who manages a voice of reason. "Howard will guide us. We must trust True Cause."

"Trust True Cause. Trust True Cause," murmur the others.

I do not chant with them. I cannot seem to think what they are thinking. Instead there is a deep ache in me that I failed to bring Jamie into True Cause. I hardly tried. And he asked all those questions so he must have been curious. Curiosity is a Positive Outsider Response. So why did I not push harder? What was I doing? But even as I think this I know, deep in the centre of me, that I knew exactly what I was doing. I did not try properly because we—The Chosen—never mix with ordinary Followers. Once Jamie had been Sealed I would have had no chances to be with him.

I hate myself as I let the thought spread and grow. I have been narrow, weak, and selfish. But it is too late for any of this now. I must take my place with the other Chosen. If I had any choices, I have burnt them away. I must live with this knowledge beyond Endtime and into Eternity.

"I love you all," I whisper.

"Love you."

"Love you."

"Love you."

"Come on." I try to keep the fear from my voice. "Howard will be waiting." I scan each face, as if I am trying to burn the memory of them into my mind, then herd them through the door.

Outside I had expected chaos, but the night is strangely quiet. We link together and walk with the other Followers who are spilling out from the barns and outhouses, and from the camp sites in the outlying fields. Everyone is moving towards Hill Park grounds. They are all calm, although some are smiling, their eyes shining as if they have been lit from the inside. I am not calm or smiling though. I am trembling. Failing.

The Watchers move amongst us. "True Cause is the true cause," they murmur. "This is not an end, it is a beginning."

"This is not an end, it is a beginning," we reply.

The gates are open and we crush through, the eleven of us pushing our way along the edges of the gathering and up to the front.

This has been practised and practised—apart from special celebrations it is the only time we ever get close to the mansion. But at Endtime Howard wants us where he can see us, and in the past I have always taken great comfort from this.

All across the grounds there are Howard's strangely shaped trees, cut and clipped so that their origins are barely recognizable. In the dark they seem like creatures that are not of this world.

Not of this world. Not of this world. Soon this world will not be of anything. I am shaking, scared, and I realize I am afraid of pain.

The mansion ahead is a shadowed bulk, its white facade tangled with the trunks of vines that have been trained along the blank face of its walls. I have the sense that it is waiting. Waiting.

There seem to be hundreds of us, all faces turned towards the house. I had not known our numbers had grown so fast and the thought of all these New Joiners who will now be Saved is stunning. It seems there is a swell of love that wraps around them and holds them all together. Nobody speaks, but in the silence their joy is like something buzzing. I am struggling to feel it too.

The huge carved doors in the centre of the mansion are reached by sixteen stone steps. In the daylight drills, I often Image myself walking up them—floating in my dress of white silk—and it hits me now that this will never happen. So many things will never happen.

Jamie. Jamie.

I try to calm my fresh wave of panic by counting the windows—twelve on each wing, four on each floor—and then another eighteen in the centre block. One top floor window, tall and arched, opens on to a curved white balcony which protrudes above the main doors. There is a flickering light in the room behind.

All around me Followers are beginning to sway. Some are chanting, the sound sweetening the chilled air. They are all so happy. Happy happy happy.

I realize suddenly that everyone is looking up, their necks craned backwards. I tilt my head, too, and what I see stills my breath.

The sky is as smooth as oil and stars skid and slide across the liquid dark. Tiny explosions boil up out of nothing. A cluster of lights burns with a slow fierce glow. A hiss of silver spills down in a spluttering shower.

"True Cause is the true cause. True Cause is the true cause."

We all grip hands. I feel Isabel's nails cut into my skin.

The stars skim faster, criss-crossing each other as they fizz through the dark. I cannot take such a terrible beauty, and I have to look away.

Suddenly there is a flood of gold lighting the balcony. The Brides have gathered there in a silent semi-circle, pale as ghosts, strangely translucent, as if they have no substance. I know them all—should know them all—but the past is a fog and it blankets my memory, muffling all their names.

And now Howard is there with them, his hands stretched out to us. His robes shine round him, and his hair is wild and spiked and almost luminous.

"This is the beginning," he calls. "The beginning of the end. But we are together. We are where we should be." There is a shake to his voice and from my close-up position I think that his whole face seems to be moving. It is as if his own private Endtime is playing itself out under his skin.

I wonder what the final moment will be. An exploding ball of fire? The earth splitting and sucking us all down? A giant wave roaring in from the sea? Maybe it will be all of these things. Isabel and Felicity are gripping me so tightly it feels that my fingers will break. I am gripping them that tightly too. Let it come. Let it come.

At the edge of the crush I see a New Joiner break away as if he thinks he can make a run for it. He fails. Two Watchers chase after him, grappling him to the ground. Then they bring him, kicking and struggling, back in. I wonder where it is he thought he was going.

"Trust in True Cause. Trust in me," Howard screams.

"Trust in True Cause. Trust in Howard," we all scream back.

"Kneel." Howard raises his arms, his robe lifting like wings. "It is better that you all kneel."

We kneel. The ground is damp and cold and it startles me that it should feel so solid. As if no one has yet told the ground that the world is ending and it is behaving as if it is just an ordinary night.

"*Tanyon sanyon connito. Tess arison vell teeomber creesoraus . . .*"

Howard's True Cause words blunt the edges of my panic and I join the chant, murmuring it over and over, an endless roll of sound. And we wait.

14

The sunrise washes across the fading dark. The spill of stars has stopped. We are still kneeling. Still waiting. Back down at the farm the cock starts crowing.

"This was a forewarning." Howard is like a statue on the balcony, his fists clenched as if he might be about to fight someone—or something. "To see if we are ready. To see how much we trust. And we have risen to the moment. We are well prepared. I know now, more than I ever have, that when Endtime comes we will walk boldly to meet it. And now, a new day has begun. We must work harder than we ever have. Get up earlier. Stay up later. There are still so many Unsaved."

"So many Unsaved. So many Unsaved."

It strikes me that Howard seems smaller in the rising light. The Brides seem small too, huddled into each other. I suppose they must be tired.

We must all be.

But above the tiredness I suddenly want to laugh with the excitement that I have a new chance. I will forget my own narrow selfishness and bring Jamie in. Everything is for a reason. I can see exactly what that means now. It is brilliant and wonderful that this new knowledge has been shown to me. Everything is clear. Washed clean. The Bad Thoughts will never haunt me again.

Howard raises his arms again. "Today will be as any other. You will all continue with whatever work you have been assigned to, but I think you will see now that every extra day before Endtime is a gift we must not waste."

"Every extra day is a gift we must not waste. Every extra day is a gift we must not waste."

Howard reaches out to us, and we all reach back. Then he steps away through the arched window, disappearing inside the mansion.

I suddenly realize the Brides have already gone. Perhaps they faded. Like my memories of them. I still cannot remember their names.

15

It is another week before I see Jamie again.

I have been lucky. So lucky. Isabel is not well and I have been given permission to collect bags of leaves for the flower pressings. And anyway, since Howard received the newest message from his Divine Writings, Shadowing is being phased out. "Cut back on Coupling Up. Success lies with Singling." He explained it to us at yesterday's Meeting, and it is to do with the new urgency about Endtime. Every extra day is a day we must not waste, and every Singling is twice as efficient as the old clumsy Shadowing.

There is a new buzz around everyone. We have started to run a lot, as if every assignment is a race. And I suppose it is. A race against time. We must be ready.

Of course, I could collect the leaves from many places, but there is only one real option for me. I am going to where Jamie might be waiting.

I am hoping. I am hoping. And I would be running there, too, except it is hard to run amongst trees and holly and over uneven ground.

A part of me thinks I should be able to be truthful about where I am going, if saving Jamie is part of the Great Plan—but there is still a whisper that tells me to be careful. I may understand this part of the picture, but it is possible that some of the Watchers will be confused about what I am doing, and nothing must go wrong. I think, as I stoop through the tunnel of branches, that he may not be here. I am hardened to that possibility this time.

I will even accept it. He will be here if he is meant to be here. And the next moment I see him, and I know it is Meant.

He is sitting on the fallen branch, his back against the trunk of the tree, a smudge of mud across his cheek which I get the sudden urge to wipe away. He is scribbling in his notebook again. I think that maybe I will be able to creep really close and surprise him, but I am not soft footed enough and my boots scrunch down on a mesh of dry twigs. Jamie looks up and smiles. Nothing more. Just smiles.

I melt. I have been thinking and thinking and thinking about him, but in every Image I have been in control, leading the conversation the way it needs to go. I have not prepared myself for melting.

"Hiya."

"Hello."

He gets up and reaches out as if he is going to hold me, but I back away. If I am here to save him I cannot get lost in him again.

"What's up?"

I stand looking at him, my grand words shrivelling to nothing.

He pushes the notebook into his pocket. "You look pretty wrecked. What's been going on?"

I collect myself and force my thoughts into a straight line. If I just talk, keep talking, I will stay on the path I need to be on. "Something happened last week. Something beautiful and terrible."

He shakes his head. "I'm sorry. I shouldn't have done it."

I am puzzled. I have no idea what he means. Keep the straight line. Keep the straight line. "Everything that happens is for a reason," I say. "It is all as it is meant to be."

He shakes his head. "It was still out of order. It's not what I meant—well, not exactly, anyway."

It takes me another moment, and then I realize he is talking about the kiss. My face flushes at the memory. And why is he thinking it was beautiful and terrible? Has it shamed him? Or is it something to do with Naomi—he shouldn't have done it because he shouldn't be hurting Naomi. An Image of Naomi comes stinging in and I struggle to block her away. Straight line. Straight line. "Not . . . what we did." I find I cannot speak the word "kiss," as if it is something dangerous. Just to sound out the letters would bring it alive again. "I mean something else. Something bigger than both of us."

"I don't get you."

I take a breath. I will not talk about Endtime yet. I have to make him understand more first. "I thought I'd never see you again . . ."

His eyes narrow and he takes a step nearer again, and this time I do not step back. "What did they do to you?"

"Nothing. Nothing." I close my eyes as he pushes my hair back behind my ears and the touch of him washes through me. If he was a river I would drown in him. I am weak and pathetic. Straight line. Straight line. I open my eyes again. "True Cause never hurts us. We are being Saved. We are lucky."

He shakes his head and sits down again, pulling

me next to him. "What makes you so sure?"

"Because everything is unfolding as it should. We have to trust what is meant to be."

He has his hand on my hand. There is such warmth that comes off him. It is hard—so hard—not to lace my fingers with his. Not to tilt my head and rest it on his shoulder.

"I . . . I knew of someone who got nabbed by your lot once. Two people. They were great. Really special . . ." He trails off, then says quickly, "They never came out. The woman cut away from her whole family. Her friends. If your place is such a great idea, why can't the Followers stay in touch with everyone they knew on the 'outside' as you put it?"

I move my hand away from his, lock it with my own. I have heard all this before. "No True Cause members are stopped from doing anything. Followers work hard for the Cause, and there is little spare time, but no one is ever Forbidden to see anyone. If the woman cut herself off, she will have had a reason."

"Like she was brainwashed?"

"Like she was happy."

For a while neither of us speaks. He breaks a stick from the branch and scratches at a mush of fungus that has mouldered along the underside. I can tell by the hunch of his shoulders that he is upset, and I am sorry. Sorry I cannot reach out to him, but I have clicked into place now. Straight line. Straight line.

"So . . . this thing that happened—that made you think you'd never see me again. What was it?"

"It was a sign. And a warning."

He raises one eyebrow and leans back against the tree again, smears of fungus caught on the tip of his stick. "Go on."

He is back in Positive Outsider Response again. Now I must get him to Second Level.

"I was scared at first. I thought it was going to be the end. We all did."

"The end of what?"

"The end of time," I say carefully. "And the path to the New Beginning."

He shakes his head and I am sure he is trying to block out his fear, so I hurry on, "It was a beautiful sight. That was what I meant by beautiful and terrible. The sky was full of stars and they were falling all round us and . . ."

He flicks the smears of fungus into the air. "You mean the meteor shower?"

"No. Not a shower. This was stars burning up and planets exploding and . . ."

"It wasn't the end of time, Elinor. It was an astronomical event. A meteor shower, like I said. I drove up to Lodge Point and watched it with a bunch of mates."

I am startled that he knows about it. I believed it was a sign for only us. I realize I do not quite understand how the sky works. I have never considered it before. And this thought gets me struggling against the tide again.

"You saw it?"

"Most of Europe did. It was a big deal. A shower like that only comes round every five hundred years."

"You mean—you knew it was coming?" This knocks me sideways. How could Outsiders have known, and not us?

"It's been hyped up in the paper for weeks."

I try to look as if I know what he is talking about, but it is just an act. We are Forbidden to read papers—even to linger near anywhere that sells newspapers can corrupt the mind.

"Were . . . were you scared?"

"Course not. It was great. There was this barbecue afterwards—hot dogs and baked spuds and stuff, and there was a funfair that kept going all night. Some of the rides were pretty wild by dawn. We had a laugh."

I think about all of our chanting and crying, the cold numbing our knees.

I think of Jamie, up at Lodge Point eating hot

dogs. Whirling about wildly on the fairground rides. Having a laugh.

Was Naomi there? Did they stand together and watch the exploding night? I have to pull myself out of these Bad Thoughts.

I am losing my track.

He touches my arm. "You've gone quiet again. What's up?"

"I just—it sounds almost like a different night. A different time altogether."

"Well, I guess if we'd all been persuaded it was the end of the world like you were, we might have put a different slant on it."

"We weren't 'persuaded.' Howard is preparing us. It's Outsiders who are wrong. Outsiders who cannot understand."

"Elinor . . . Elinor. Your Howard is scary. Don't you ever even *try* to question what goes on?"

I am being battered by his words. "Nothing goes *on*. We're trying to save people. As many as we can. There's no time to waste. Can't you see . . ."

He grips my wrist, pulls me round and his face is close up to mine, but now his eyes are not warm, but narrowed and angry. "Listen to you. *Listen* to yourself. You're like an effing tape recorder. Can't you even begin to think for yourself?"

I stare back at him. I am shaking. Really shaking. I have been blocked by Outsiders before, but the things he is saying are scaring me. I do not want to hear. I *must* not hear. I have to pull back the memory of that washed-clean moment in the grounds last week. The moment when I banished Bad Thoughts for ever.

He sighs suddenly, his eyes softening, taking hold of my shoulders. "Sorry sorry sorry. I'm push-ing too hard. Expecting too much. It's just—this is all so slow."

I am not certain what he means, but I cannot look at him and I twist my face away. "I need to go." My stomach is turning as if I have swallowed smears of fungus. "I've still got some leaves to collect."

He drops his arms, and there is a long silence. An endless space between us. "Look—I don't want to rock you like this. I just hate the way Howard forces you to live."

"Howard doesn't force anyone to do anything. We all do things because we want to."

He is trying to damage me. Dangerous and devi-ous. Dangerous and devious. True Cause is the true cause. True Cause is the true cause.

"Shit, Elinor." He shakes his head. "Okay. Okay."

I stand up. He stands with me, and I manage to make my eyes meet his.

"Don't," he whispers. "Don't leave like this."

"I have to."

He nods then. "I'm sorry. I've . . . I've messed everything up. I only wanted . . ." His sentence trails away, and I wonder, for a moment, what it is he "only wanted," but I make myself think that it does not matter. Why should it?

I turn and walk away, a part of me still listening for him, aching for him to come after me.

I am failing. Failing. Bad Thoughts. Bad Thoughts.

And I have not saved him. I cannot save him.

Is this how it is meant to be?

16

I actually slept. But now, awake with "Beware and be wary" ringing out from the loudspeaker in the yard, I know I have dreamt of him. In the dream he had his back to me and he was talking to a small boy who looked familiar. I think perhaps the boy is a New Joiner's son, but I cannot Image which one.

I feel empty.

"We've got to sort through the New Joiners' Clearings for the weekend market. Howard has set those new targets. We must price everything higher." Isabel sounds frantic as I climb down from my bunk. I can tell she has been running this through her head for half the night.

I struggle for a moment, trying to connect with

everything she is saying. "It's all right. There's plenty of time. We're assigned to the Clearings barn straight after the Meeting."

"I know, but what if the Meeting runs on again, like it has done over the last few days."

"Then we'll work through the night." The idea of working through the night does not seem so terrible. At least it will stop me from dreaming.

But watching Isabel get up slowly from her bunk, her back stooped and her face whited out and hollow, I think that she should not even work through the morning. "Why don't you stay in bed again?" I say. "Felicity and Imogen are assigned to the Clearings too. I'm sure between the three of us we'll get it all done."

Isabel shakes her head. "A Carer came to see me yesterday. He says this tiredness is necessary at the moment. Lots of us are feeling it, but every day is a gift we must not waste. I need to be stronger in my mind. And look . . ." She rolls up the sleeve of her nightdress. "I've got this rash. The Carer said it was Bad Thoughts leaking out. So Bad Thoughts must be coming in even though I'm not aware of them. I need to concentrate more. Concentrate. Concentrate."

She is right, of course. We must all concentrate. Especially me.

I have to shake all these Jamie thoughts out and

get on with being who I am. But he is under my skin when I cleanse. He is in my head as I eat the rice and nut breakfast. As I walk towards Star Temple the memory of him jars through every step.

Isabel begins coughing on the walk, and we have to stop while she gets her breath again.

"I'm fine now," she says at last, leaning against me. But we move on very slowly after that, and she has to stop every few paces.

We take our places and as I watch the others fil-ing in I suddenly notice, in amongst the New Joiners, a face I recognize. It is Della—the woman from the park. She has Alice with her, but the twins will be kept in the crèche. Howard holds separate Meetings for the babies.

Seeing Della brings on the thought that I must be doing something right. I am still saving Outsiders. But the thought has no shape, as if the edges of it are blunt-ed. I am saving Outsiders, but I have not saved Jamie.

I have not saved Jamie.

Howard comes through as our singing starts up, his eyes burning anger. I feel my stomach twist. Something new has happened. Something Bad. Rebecca nudges me from behind, and I see that beyond Howard, just to the right of the chamber door,

Rael and another Watcher have just placed a glass tank of water. I glance back at Rebecca and shrug, and she looks as startled by this as she does by the tank.

Shrugging. We never shrug. It is an Outsider gesture. I look to the front again quickly, wondering what else of Jamie's I may have caught. Have bits of him become me? Have bits of me become him?

Our song drops to a low hum.

"There is no one we can trust!" Howard jerks his head from side to side as if there are demons that only he can see. "Dark dangers are swimming through the waters of betrayal."

"Swimming through the waters of betrayal," we all whisper. "Swimming through the waters of betrayal."

I realize Howard is holding something—a newspaper. I am shocked that this should have been brought into Star Temple, and I stare in horror as if toxic vibrations are somehow going to shudder up out of it and pollute us all.

Then I think of Jamie's meteorite display, and my Endtime. I realize my nails are digging into the skin of my hands and I am suddenly confused again.

"There are new lies. Outsider lies. And I am drowning in grief that this Betrayal came from within." Howard shakes his head.

There is a long silence.

He stares ahead and I think he may be deep in a meditative trance. He enters this state sometimes, but usually only at Healings, when he speaks in the tongues that his messengers send him.

Time passes. I listen to the phut of the candles, and watch the pale sunlight that filters down onto the mosaic floor.

I begin to worry that there is not time for all this standing. Every new day is a gift we must not waste. Every new day is a gift we must not waste.

And then I think that this must be a Bad Thought because everything happens for a reason. I must trust Howard to know what the right thing is.

And suddenly Howard does seem to know, because he snaps back suddenly, "I call for witness Follower Caroline Markham."

A woman from the second row of the Followers raises her arm. "That's me."

Howard walks across, his hand reaching out for hers. "Join me."

Once she has climbed the steps, he faces her.

"Things have been complicated for you recently, I have been told."

She nods. Her hands are clasped in front of her and her head is slightly bowed, the way Followers must always stand before Howard.

"Tell us your story."

"My husband has left True Cause. He told me the morning after the Endtime warning that he was going to go."

"And you didn't try to stop him?"

"I begged him to stay. Begged him to talk to one of the Counsellors. I shouted and cried. I got others to speak to him and a band of us ran after him down the road . . ."

"Why didn't he listen?"

"He has a strong mind. It's hard to shake him from his point of view."

"So . . ." there is a sharper edge to Howard's voice, ". . . you are saying that someone of a strong mind would leave True Cause?"

"I . . . no. I meant stupidly strong. Stubborn. Like a donkey."

"Donkeys are not so stupid. What is your husband's name?"

"Andy. Andrew."

"Andy. Andrew. Andy. Andrew." Howard mimics her wavering tone and then thrusts the toxic newspaper in her face. "This—on the front page. Read it."

She begins to scan the words although I am sure she cannot see it properly because she is shaking so much.

"Out loud. Out loud. So all can hear."

She speaks out loud, although not *actually* loud and I strain to catch her words. *"New exposure on the cons behind the True Cause cult. A frank confession by ex-cultist Andrew Markham . . ."*

Howard is wincing at every word, as if he is being stung.

Caroline Markham stops in mid-sentence. "I can't . . ."

"Read on," Howard snaps round at her. "We should all hear this. We should all hear the tide of lies that is lapping at our feet."

She reads on:

"In a climate where mainstream religion has lost its grip, cults like True Cause, based just outside Braxbury, are reaping a spiritual harvest. Man, it seems, needs a belief system, and if society no longer imposes a religious framework on life, then he will find his own. Andy Markham, who was drawn into the cult with his wife Caroline only six months ago, tells how Followers—mainly made up of society's losers and dropouts—are manipulated into giving up their lives—and their minds—to the 'Master' Howard Reiki."

Howard cuts her off. "Losers and dropouts . . ." His eyes are black slits as he points to an egg-headed man with glasses. ". . . You, my friend—tell us—were you begging on the streets before you joined True Cause?"

The man clears his throat importantly. "I was a Financial Adviser."

"Did you live in a damp basement, squatting with drug addicts and alcoholics?"

"I had a four-bedroomed detached property on the outskirts of London. I'm here because I chose to be here. In those days I had everything—and nothing." He presses his heart with his hand and looks round at everyone. "Nothing in here—in my soul. True Cause has given my life both meaning and virtue."

"Praise True Cause," says Howard.

"Praise True Cause. Praise True Cause," everybody murmurs.

Howard moves along, pointing this time at a young woman. "And you—forgive my crude tongue, but were you a prostitute polluting your soul to satisfy the sin of cheap lust? Or some drab, down-at-heel housewife driven crazy by a deranged partner from whom you were desperate to escape?"

She giggles, and glances at the broad-shouldered man next to her. "I came with my husband. We sold up the country hotel that Paul inherited because we were tired of the small-mindedness and immorality of so many of our guests. We have never been happier than we are in True Cause."

"Praise True Cause. Praise True Cause."

"So . . . losers? Dropouts?" Howard opens his arms as if he would embrace us all. "I don't think so, my friends. Even the word cult here is deceptive. The word cult is from the Latin *cultus,* meaning worship or ritual. Are Outsiders claiming there is something wrong with the practice of worship or ritual? And do they themselves not surround themselves with false idols—footballers on salaries of thirty thousand pounds a week. Pop heroes pounding out filth and scum and corrupting young minds. These are the Gods that Outsiders worship. These are their hollow 'Masters.' And I . . . I am offering salvation beyond Endtime—not for me—but for all of you. For as many as I can fit in this temple. And when we fill this temple I shall build another. And another. There will be Star Temples across the land. Across the world. Except this—" He snatches the newspaper from Caroline Markham and thrusts it high into the air. "This is run by the demons who seek to destroy us. True Cause must do more than swim through the murk of this menace. True Cause must learn to fly."

We are led into the Chant of Tongues by Rael, who steps forward and releases a white dove into the air.

As the bird flutters noisily above us, we whisper and wail and sing and shout, all of our sounds mingling, meaning nothing and everything.

The Chant of Tongues drains away to a hum. Howard turns again to Caroline Markham. "What do you say to all this?"

"I'm sorry."

"We are all to blame." He takes both her hands and holds her gently. "None of us have been vigilant enough. While we are diving amongst the delights of our coral gardens, we must learn to stay watchful for sharks." He shakes his head, pulling her closer. "And he has left you with a child, this Andy Andrew?"

"Our new baby. Just six weeks. Bella."

"And would you agree that Andy Andrew should Receive Punishment as he has betrayed True Cause—and you and the beautiful baby Bella—in this way?"

Caroline Markham sniffs and nods.

"Is any punishment too harsh?"

She seems to draw back for a moment, and Howard raises his eyebrows slightly. It is a slight, slight movement, but for some reason I flinch.

"No. None."

"And he loves his daughter? He loves the little baby Bella?" Howard has his arm around her shoulders but his voice does not match the gesture and I find I am leaning forward as if there is something more I should see that is not quite clear. There is something in his voice. In his face. He is like the stranger—the Unknown—that my Bad Thoughts have sometimes Imaged him to be.

"I . . . I'm not sure," Caroline Markham replies at last.

"Not sure? Not sure that he loves her? So this Andy Andrew is a man who does not love his tiny defenceless daughter and would not want to protect her with his life."

"He does love her . . . it's just . . ."

"A man who believes this . . . this drivel that we are being tainted with . . ." He forms the words slowly, shaking his head. ". . . And yet still leaves the fruit of his own loins in the hands of what he is claiming is an evil cult? He must at least be a man who is coldhearted. Coldhearted and dangerous. Don't you think?"

"Coldhearted and dangerous." Caroline Markham's voice is getting quieter and quieter.

"Beyond Endtime my Brides will bear me children. They will be special children, endowed with great gifts. But no child who is not mine will be gifted in this way. Not exactly this way. Or do you think they could?"

"No."

"And why is that?"

Her voice lifts to make her answer into a question, as if she is uncertain what the right answer might be again. "Because—they have your genes, and it's your genes that make them special?"

My unease is growing, as if there is a storm hovering and I am waiting for the first crack of thunder.

"So—does it not follow that a child who is the product of someone who is coldhearted and dangerous will develop those genes too? Will she not be in danger of growing up in the same mould?"

"I—Andy. Perhaps he wasn't bad. Just confused."

"But just now you agreed that your Andy Andrew was coldhearted and dangerous. Are you confused too? Are both poor baby Bella's parents weak willed and riddled with indecision?"

Caroline is shaking her head.

"Maybe the baby Bella Markham will also grow up to be weak willed and riddled with indecision. Do we want that for True Cause Followers of the future? Should we risk it?"

He steps back and looks round at all of us.

"Should we risk it? Should we risk it?" The murmur runs round the temple, but I do not think that everyone joins in. For the first time ever, I see that there are Followers who look away.

The door to the Chamber opens and Rael appears. He is carrying a baby. It is impossible to see the baby's face because she is swaddled in so many blankets and shawls, but from Caroline's sharp intake of breath I can tell that it must be Bella. I feel cold inside. Ice cold.

Howard takes the blanketed bundle from Rael and walks towards the tank. "We should wash this child clean of its parents' failures," he cries.

With a shout that is half animal he plunges the bundle into the tank of water.

Caroline, now screaming, is held back by Rael.

It is terrible to watch. Worse even than Meryl.

The baby seems to struggle as Howard presses her onto the bottom of the tank. Tiny bubbles fizz up to the surface. The blankets unravel slightly, and one corner flaps strangely with a slow rhythmic beat.

I want to scream, too, but I do not dare.

I cannot believe this is happening. In front of us—right in front of us—Howard is drowning a tiny baby and no one is running forward to stop him. Including me. And then suddenly Howard steps backwards, lifting the bundle out of the water. The shawls drip long lines across Star Temple floor.

There is no hope. I know this. Everyone must know it. Bella has been in the water too long.

Slowly, Howard begins to part the folds of the dripping blankets. He turns the bundle to face us and I cannot bear what I am going to have to look at—but like the others I crane to see what I do not want to see. And then—when it is first revealed I struggle to take it in. Grey and silver. Its rubber mouth giving slow tired gasps and its round strange eyes staring out at nothing. It is only a fish.

"From my ponds," smiles Howard, his face glowing as he looks round at us all. "I have hundreds of these. I've nurtured them. Watched them grow and flourish, as we in True Cause will grow and flourish."

"We in True Cause will grow and flourish. We in True Cause will grow and flourish."

I open and close my mouth, fishlike, but I do not speak the words. I cannot speak the words. Or maybe it is that I will not speak the words.

Howard the Stranger. Howard the Unknown.

Rael nods towards the chamber door, and a Watcher appears with an identical bundle of shawls, only this time the miniature fists punching the air are clear to see, and the tiny thin wail that echoes round the temple mingles with the joyful rise of our True Cause song.

Caroline Markham stumbles forward, grabbing her baby, sobbing and clutching her to her chest.

"You see," Howard says, smiling first at her, and then up and around at us all, "I am here to save, not to destroy. But we must be wary. Ever wary. That is our lesson for today."

"Wary. Ever wary." Caroline Markham is kneeling, rocking, before him. "Thank you. Thank you for everything."

He touches the crown of her head. "We must celebrate this beautiful moment."

I take Isabel's hand. Or at least, I go to take her hand. But her grip loosens as I hold it and she slides away from me, crumpling onto the floor.

"Isabel? Isabel?" My voice is a frantic hiss.

Two Watchers move in to gather her up. Her face is white stone, one arm hanging limp and her hair falling in long silvery reeds.

I try to follow the Watcher but he shakes his head. "You need to be here," he commands. "Nothing must be missed."

Felicity moves over into the space where Isabel was standing. I realize the other Chosen have shifted their places slightly too. It is already as if Isabel was never there.

17

"Find yourselves a comfortable position. Some way you can be relaxed. Let the peace flow round you and across you. Let it warm the soul within." The Counsellor walks around the barn, touching each of us in turn.

We have come straight from the Meeting. "Where's Isabel?" I call softly.

"Just let the peace flow round you." The Counsellor squats beside me. "There's nothing to worry about."

"I didn't understand about the fish." I have to say this. The sentence bubbles up out of me and seems to float in the air.

"I thought it was funny." Imogen giggles.

Rebecca giggles. Then everyone giggles. I think I am giggling, too, although I am not sure. And I am still worrying about Isabel.

"Sssssh now. Ssssssh. Howard is looking after us. Trust him. Trust Howard," murmurs the Counsellor.

"Trust him. Trust Howard," we say.

I try to drown the Unknown Howard Image that swims through my mind. Most of the others sit cross-legged with their eyes shut. Felicity is face down. I, for some reason, have suddenly curled tight, my knees tucked into my chest.

"You are lucky. So lucky." The Counsellor is walking amongst us. I can hear his soft tread across the floor. Outside, rain rattles down onto the tin roof.

"Lucky. So lucky." We sound distant. We are distant.

"True Cause was not an accident. A chance. Not any more than the sun and the moon and the million zillion stars in the sky. You—Howard's chosen—are part of the Great Plan."

"Part of the Great Plan. Part of the Great Plan . . ."

I focus my thoughts on the sun and the moon and the million zillion stars and then I remember the night the stars fell. The meteorite display.

Think for yourself, Elinor. Think for yourself.

Howard the Stranger. Howard the Unknown.

And I am thinking for myself. Or trying to.

"Everything we do in True Cause . . ."

I have stopped echoing the Counsellor. Stopped even listening. I am still struggling to understand the fish, and to take my ideas somewhere new.

But then I realize—maybe it is not new I want— maybe I want old. Maybe I have to go back back back. But where to? And why?

Think for yourself, Elinor. Think for yourself.

". . . relax your minds and trust me. You have been Chosen . . ."

I think suddenly of Cornish pasties. Rows and rows and rows of them.

". . . *Cant any neary. Cant any neary . . .*"

I am slipping. It is so easy to slip.

Think for yourself, Elinor. Think for yourself.

And suddenly a memory comes rolling up as if it has loomed out of a fog. I lock very still and my breathing slows. I know, without knowing, that this is important. Concentrate. Concentrate.

I see a woman in a chair. She has her back to me and a man with a shock of ginger hair is hovering over her. He is talking in a tone that is hurried. Urgent. On my Bad Bad days when I forget to concentrate I have seen this scene before, although I have, until now, always pushed it away . . .

"You're not thinking, not feeling." The man squats down in front of the woman, taking her hands in his. "You look lost. You are lost. But I'm going to bring you back. I'm going to make you feel something."

There is no reaction from the woman. No movement. I have the sense that I am not just watching this in my head, but that I am really there, although I am well hidden, crouched behind a pale cream curtain. There is green carpet on the floor and the fibres in it scratch my knees.

I am not used to carpet.

"You're like a zombie. If you would only look at yourself properly—but then Howard bans mirrors, doesn't he." The ginger man straightens up again and shakes his head.

I can barely hear the woman's response, although I know the pattern of what she replies. "The outer form is nothing and nowhere. We learn to love the soul within. We learn to love the soul within."

"You make me so angry," the man suddenly shouts and I flinch. "Your pupils are dilated. Your veins are sticking out. Your skin is pale and riddled with rashes. You think the rashes are the devil eating his way out, don't you, Maria? And you think

I'm the devil, too. Don't you? Don't you?"

The woman does not rise to meet his anger. Instead her reply is distant and flat. "True Cause is the true cause. True Cause is the true cause."

"I'm not leaving here." The man's tone is stubborn now. "I will stay here for as long as it takes to get you to talk to me. Think for yourself, Maria."

"Leave me alone. Please leave me alone. True Cause is the true cause. True Cause is the true cause."

"Stop it, Maria." He has softened again. "We've got you out of there now. You don't have to trot out all those empty phrases. You don't have to block your mind with endless chants."

"True Cause is the true cause. True Cause is the true cause."

"Remember your family. Not the golden and glorious True Cause family but your real family. The people you knew from Outside."

"I need to save them." She seems to tense slightly, and for the first time there is some spark in what she says. "I have to find a way to bring them in."

"It's not them who need saving, Maria, it's you. Your friend David has paid hundreds to get me here. You remember David, don't you, Maria? Don't you? Don't you?"

Maria shifts her shoulders as if she is trying to

readjust something heavy and uncomfortable that is weighing on her.

"And his son. They both cared about you. Don't you think they miss you?" He fishes in his pocket. "This is a photograph of you all at the beach last summer. It's David and his son. You and your little girl. You all look so happy. It was one of those magical days, wasn't it? Think for yourself, Maria. Think for yourself."

He forces the picture on her and at first I think that she will only crumple it up, but from the tilt of her head I realize that she is looking at it. Staring at it. She stays like that for a long time.

And then she starts to cry.

She slumps forward, her head in her hands, and her body is racked by gasping sobs that seem to wrench out from the core of her.

The sound tears at me. I want to run to her, to be near her, but before I can grapple my way out from behind the curtain the door is forced open and two Watchers burst in and grab them both.

"He's got through to her," one of the Watchers is shouting, and he sounds scared. "We're too fucking late."

"Just get them away. Howard will sort it." I hear the voice of the second one and I look at him with a cold shock. I know him. It is Rael. And as he wrestles the ginger man from the room he calls back, "Find the kid. She must be in here somewhere."

A minute later I am pulled from behind the curtains where I have curled tight with my knees tucked to my chest and I am whispering over and over, "Mummy. Mummy. I want Mummy."

And then the whole scene fades and I am still in the barn. The Counsellor is saying, "We must do what we must do. True Cause is everything. Howard is everything."

"True Cause is everything. Howard is everything."

I curl even tighter. I do not know what to do because I am crying and the Chosen never cry. Why would we? Why should we? But tears are flooding my face and I am screaming and screaming but only in my head—only silently because the Counsellor must not hear.

Mummy.

Mummy.

18

I cannot sleep. I am too restless. I have been rocked by this Sudden Sight—the idea of a Mother. Mummy. Although it is not a Prediction. It is a picture of the past. I am trying to Image her face, but nothing comes. I have the sense of her, but not the vision. I wonder where she is now? Does she think of me? Does it matter? There are other things too.

More ghosted memories seem to press forward from the dark at the back of my mind. I wish my head would stop hurting and I could think more clearly, but every time I try and clear some space all the True Cause chants and songs push back in and block it up again.

I am lucky. So lucky.

Howard Our Master.

Howard who Saves.

What was today about, with Caroline Markham and the fish? Baby. Fish. Baby. Fish. Something scared me but I have forgotten what it was.

Where is Isabel? And Meryl? I must not think about them. Everything is for the best.

Necessary. Necessary.

I am lucky. So lucky.

Howard Our Master.

Howard who Saves.

There is no one to talk to. No one.

19

There is a struggling sun, and the market is busier than it was last month.

"Mummy, can I have that china doll?"

"It's an ornament, sweetheart. Not something you can really play with. How about this little pink elephant?"

I watch the girl pick up the elephant and press its trunk against her freckled cheek. I watch the mother smiling down at her.

Was I ever that little? Did my mother—Maria—smile at me like that? I have not really thought about the happiness of Outsiders before. How could the Unsaved, with their narrow material lives, ever understand happiness? But these two look happy.

That is what floods my mind as I watch them together. They look happy. Is there a difference between believing you're happy and actually being happy. How do you know which one is which?

Howard Our Master. Howard the Unknown. How do I know which Howard is which?

Bad thoughts. Bad thoughts. Just demons in my head. Of course I know. Of course. Of course.

"How much?" The mother's question jolts me back to the moment.

"Five pounds." I would like to gift it to them. I would like to keep their happiness growing. But this thinking is muddling me again. Surely I should just be trying to save them?

The mother hands me a five-pound note and they go off together, the little girl dancing the pink elephant by its ears.

I am suddenly scared by the idea that Jamie might be here. He probably knows this is our day. We do this every fourth Sunday. A lot of Outsiders come here especially because of us—dealers and collectors sometimes buy up a whole stall. It always fascinates me the way all these "things" go back out on to different shelves and cupboards. How do Outsiders make sense of their world?

Opposite me, on the ground by the hot dog van,

a scrunch of tinfoil catches the sun and glitters like a jewel. Tinfoil is part of Outsider technology. It does not burn. Does not decay. It is a Bad Thing. A Bad Thing. But it is still beautiful. *Beautiful.* A small gang of teenagers wander past. My stomach knots tight—but they are not Jamie. Why should they be? Why would Jamie come looking for me?

"Can you spare me any coins?" Imogen, who is manning the stall next to me, calls across. "Everyone's giving me notes this morning."

I check in my money bag but I have mainly notes too. "If Felicity takes over here I can go and get some. Rebecca and Rachel have got a stall down near the entrance, and Elizabeth is around selling The Book somewhere."

"Fine. Felicity . . . ?" Imogen turns as Felicity staggers out with a box of china from the back of their van. "Can you do Elinor's stall for ten minutes? We need change."

"Of course." Felicity puts the box down and crosses over to me.

"I won't be long," I tell her. I have not expected this—this chance to walk off on my own—and for a moment the memory flashes back of that time when I went looking for snowdrops. And then I remember that Jamie was not there and he will never be there

138

again and even if he was it would only make me sad to see him. There is nothing to say.

I walk quickly. A few Outsiders nudge each other and stare or whisper, but I just ignore them. I scan the stalls for Rebecca and Rachel. It is crowded today—the sun has brought everyone out—and I jostle my way through the crush.

"Hey." Someone falls into step beside me. "Remember me?"

I turn, startled, and Naomi is there, jangling her wrist in my face—she is still wearing the bracelet. I think that it could not have been that naff.

"Are you doing okay?"

"Yes. Fine, thank you." I feel awkward, pale and plain against her colours and curves. The outer form is nothing and nowhere. We learn to love the soul within. We learn to love the soul within. She has red glints in her hair and her eyes are lined with a gingery brown crayon that sweeps out from the corners. I wonder if Jamie thinks she is beautiful. I wonder if he has ever told her.

"Jamie's about," she says suddenly. "He drove me up here."

I panic, thinking she has seen him in my thoughts. Do Outsiders have Sudden Sight?

"He would have come over to your stall, but he

was chicken. He reckoned you might throw a wobbly if he just appeared. He's been worried about you, though."

Chicken? Throw a wobbly? I have no idea what she is talking about, but Jamie has been worrying about me and my heart thumps harder with the idea of it. Even though I will not go it is enough that he has had me in his head.

We pass a stall selling videos and I recognize a Watcher who is pretending to be interested in them.

It jolts me. I ought to get going. Find Rebecca's stall. Get the change. Get back.

"You matter to Jamie. You know that, don't you?"

"I . . ." I hesitate.

"It'll be brilliant if you come and say 'hi.' He'll be made up." She is walking with her head low, as if we are whispering secrets. I suppose we are.

I wonder what she means. Is he wearing makeup? Is he in an Outsider play or something? But whatever it is, I do not quite understand why she would want to take me to him. I realize, with that hard spiked stab, that I would not want to take him to her.

"Of course I'll come and say 'high,'" I say. "He matters to me too."

20

He is buying a compact disc. I know what they are, but have never listened to the sounds they make. Only sold them.

"You've had your hair cut." My voice is shaky. I am shaky. His dark hair is bristly on the top. I want to touch it. I want to touch him. He is wearing a denim jacket and a sun-yellow shirt and his moss-green eyes are flecked gold.

"I'll get going," says Naomi.

I had forgotten about her.

"Sure." He nods at her and I have the sense of a link between them that I do not want to know about.

She flicks her fingers at us both. "Catch you later, then. Text me."

Text me. *Cant any neary. Cant any neary.* Outsiders have their secret language, too. As she goes off he takes my arm. I need to tell him to drop it, that there are Watchers around, but I am dazed by his touch and I do not want him to move away.

"Have you been all right?" I manage at last.

"Sure. You?"

The question disturbs me. How have I been? Things have happened but I am not sure what they are. The ghosted memories push through again but it is all a fuzzed muddle. There are things I must not think about. My task is to save Jamie. That is the main thing. The only thing. "I'm fine, thank you," I say.

He gives a half laugh and shakes his head. "You reckon? Look—just stick with me for a bit. We'll find somewhere to talk."

Stick with me. Stick with me.

He guides me past a fruit stall. A pet care stall. A stall selling meat with headless carcasses hanging from hooks. I am sticking like glue.

We dip behind a children's blow-up castle. Behind the wall of inflated orange, children are jumping and squealing. I can hear their shouts as they leap and land. Thump squeal. Thump squeal. Someone starts crying and a woman's voice calls out,

"It's all right, Lucy. Mummy's here. Miall—stop jumping on her."

Mummy. Maria. Could I tell Jamie about that? Would he understand?

There is a mound of old tyres blotched with dusty yellow lichen and grown over with ivy and brambles. Jamie clears the spiked branches away and we sit on the tyres even though they are damp.

"I was crap to you last time. I let you down."

I stare at my hands. Now I have him so close, and to myself, all my words have dried up.

I wish I had The Book with me. It would give me something to focus on. If I could just get him to take it away and read it . . .

He is watching me, and he looks so sad.

"I want to help you," I say suddenly.

I try to smile but the look wavers and fades. He leans forward and puts his arm round me. "I know you do."

I should say more—this should be my chance—but before I can start he lifts my chin and turns my face to his.

There is the longest, longest moment and then suddenly he kisses me. I feel his lips against mine and I am shaking. He is shaking. But we do not stop. Our teeth bump and he whispers sorry and I whisper sorry for what, because I do not know what else to say, and he tightens his arms around me and we stay locked there, pressed together on the tyres, and we still do not stop.

Behind us there is the thump thump squeal thump thump squeal of the bouncing children but they are distant in another world and we grip tighter. Tighter. It is wrong, it is a Bad Thing, except it doesn't feel wrong and Bad. It feels wonderful, wonderful and I think I will just take this one wonderful moment and after that I will save him. After that . . .

. . . And then he pulls away. "We mustn't. It isn't right," he says. "I'm always letting you down . . ."

I sit up, dazed, as if he has emptied dirty water over me.

What am I doing? I am so weak. Disgustingly weak. But there's still time. I can turn this round. I brush down my hair with my hands and switch on my brightest Spread-the-Word smile and act as if the kissing has not happened. "Do you ever think about what life means? What it's really about? Do you ever . . ."

"Don't." He grips my wrist so hard that it hurts. "You've been messed up. You've had that crap fed into you for years and years. But I can't believe there isn't still some spark of who you really were.

144

However deep it goes. However scary it feels."

His words bounce out at me, as if they're knocking me out of shape. For a moment I want to let them punch their way through my skin. Land somewhere. Settle. But then duty rushes in and I stand up, twisting away from his grip. "You're not ready." I battle to believe what I am saying. If I can get this right, all the Bad Thoughts will go away. "That's why I can't reach you. You're not ready to hear the Truth."

He stands too. "One of us isn't ready, Elinor, but it isn't me." He throws his hands out, like someone who has nothing left. "Just go back through the stuff I've said. Have a proper look round at that prison camp you reckon is paradise. Try and work out why your Howard bloke swans about in a limo while the rest of you rattle round in clapped-out vans. Why you're all half starved. Why you're not trusted with even simple things like choosing your own clothes. Why Followers who don't agree with your True Cause trash—or Followers who get sick—just suddenly disappear. And if it all starts to make sense— proper Outsider sense I mean—then ring me."

He drops his hands down again, gives me one last, hard look, then strides away. I notice he pulls his mobile telephone from his pocket as he goes. He must be ringing her. Naomi. Two seconds after me he is ringing her. I realize I am shaking and I slump back down onto the tyres because my legs are liquid and I am not sure I can stand. I did my best. He can go to Naomi and they can both be chickens and throw wobblies together and they will not be Saved, not either of them, and I do not care do not care do not care.

Someone touches my shoulder very gently. I close my eyes. He has come back. The anger drains out and I am washed with relief.

"So there you are. We've got everyone out looking for you." My eyes startle open and I am staring up into milk-pale eyes. It is not Jamie. It is Rael.

PART TWO

21

"You're lucky. So lucky." We are standing by the dress rack and Imogen is watching the female Carer lace the ties at the back of my dress.

I look down at the beaded silk bodice, and the skirt that falls from my waist in a white cascade. The silk is ice against my skin.

I Image the army of New Joiners who cut and sewed. I see them stitching the tiny crystal beads. I see them embroidering the faint True Cause stars. It strikes me that we must have had to walk a lot of streets, sell a lot of books, set up a lot of stalls—just to make this dress.

But of course it is the Right Thing. The Right

Thing. We are doing it for Howard, and Howard is doing so much for us.

Imogen fusses with the skirt of her own simple white dress. It has been adapted for the day, but hangs loose and is a touch too short. My dress has been specially made, but the other Chosen wear the same ones over and over, at least until the seams split or the hems tear beyond repair.

The other Chosen are not here. They will already be kneeling inside Star Temple, meditating on my Glorious Future. Except for Felicity. Felicity is asleep in her bunk because she hasn't been well.

There will be other Followers in Star Temple, but no New Joiners. There are some things New Joiners are not ready to know.

A car draws up outside. "This is it." Imogen lowers the veil down over my face, and hugs me hard. "I love you," she says. "And I'll miss you. We all will."

I smile from behind the white gauze. "It'll be your turn soon enough."

"But it's over a year before my time comes." Her voice is flat, but it picks up as she says suddenly, "Unless he calls me early, like he did with you. You're lucky. So lucky."

"Lucky. So lucky." I do not know why I have been called early. It is not in line with Outsider law, and Howard is usually rigid about not breaking their rules. Breaking their rules just gives them a way to get at us. Excuses to come snooping round.

"Your flowers." Imogen hands me the clasp of white lilies that we collected earlier this morning. It is normally the job of the Shadow to make the bouquet, but no one new has been moved up for me—I am still linked with Imogen and Felicity.

It was hard gathering lilies in the wood. The trees still seemed touched with the time I was there with Jamie, as if we had left all those moments behind and they were waiting for us to go back and reclaim them. But I must stop these memories. It will not help to be weakened again. Jamie brought me Bad Thoughts. He tried to lead me from the path, and I was haunted so for a while I followed. But not anymore. The Counsellor has shown me this. I have sung and chanted and swayed and loved and the demons will not dance through me again. I look down at the lilies. "These are lovely. You must have worked hard."

The Carer walks to the door and checks outside. The car engine is still running and the smell of the exhaust blows in on us. "It's time," she says, coming back over to me. "Are you ready?"

I walk slowly through the shed where I have

lived since I was first Chosen, and stop by my bunk. I have a sudden urge to touch the frame, grab on to it, as if by holding it I will remember it better. But why do I want to remember? I am moving on to my Glorious Future. "I'm ready."

Imogen steps behind me and lifts the train of my dress.

"True Cause is the true cause." The Carer stands aside as I pass her on my way out to the car.

"True Cause is the true cause," I reply.

At every step I can feel the cobbles press through the soles of the white silk shoes, and it hurts. The hurting surprises me. Nothing should hurt me on my Bonding day.

The Watcher who is driving is already standing by the open back door.

"True Cause is the true cause," he says, as I dip my head and climb inside.

"True Cause is the true cause."

It is strange in the car. There is a perfumed smell that sticks in my nostrils and my throat. The seats are too soft. The engine too smooth. I missed my time as Shadow to the Bride because of what happened to Meryl, so I have not had the training run that Imogen is getting now. I sit in the centre of the too-soft back seat, my dress spreading round me.

Imogen holds my hand. The darkened windows seem to tint the passing fields, making them dull. Depressed. Along the far side runs the line of trees that edges the wood. I will not look. I will not look.

"Don't do that," Imogen whispers. I jump because I think she means "don't think like that"—because she has caught my thoughts—but she is looking at my lap. I have been picking at the petals of a lily and have stripped it open. A tiny white heart nestles in the centre of it. I ease the heart out with my thumbnail and lay it on my palm, sorry that I have exposed it. Sorry I cannot keep it safe.

The limousine slides to a halt outside Star Temple and the Watcher comes round to let us out.

"True Cause is the true cause."

"True Cause is the true cause."

The golden door is open and I can hear the other Chosen singing—only the Chosen can sing at a Bonding. All these girls—these friends—I have grown up with. They sound so young. They are so young. I cannot understand why, but I want to cry. But then, without even knowing that my silk-clad feet have been moving, I am inside, my hand holding on to Rael who has stepped forward to escort me to the front. Imogen is behind me, carrying the train of the dress.

Howard stands at the front, shimmering in his silver Bonding robe.

I walk towards him. The air in the temple chokes with the scent of lilies.

And as I reach Howard I seem suddenly to stand outside myself, to watch as if the girl beside him in the magical beaded dress is someone else. It is just some stranger murmuring the True Cause promises, letting him seal his palm against hers.

The Chosen raise their voices in song again.

Howard and the stranger are joined beyond Endtime.

He lifts her veil, and it is as if the movement jerks me back into my body again. I have to look at him. The skin on his face is sallow and yellowed. His cheeks are sunken and there are lines pulling out from his eyes and his mouth. Amongst the silver blond of his hair there are deadened streaks of grey. Why had I never seen that he is so old?

Jamie. Jamie.

I crush my fingers tightly around the stems of the lilies. Build a fence. Keep him out. Keep him out.

The voices of the Chosen rise higher. Lifting my hair back from my face Howard marks me with the Dust of Destiny. I feel the shape of the W as it is drawn onto my forehead.

I smile, the way that all the Brides before me have smiled. "True Cause is the true cause," I murmur. "True Cause is the true cause."

But I have shivered at his touch, and I can feel the W like something numbing. Like my skin traced with ice.

Now Howard's hand is gripping mine and it is as rough as dry leaves. Memories of Jamie blast through me. I Image my mother crying, and the bearded man. *Think for yourself, Maria. Think for yourself.*

I will not remember. I must not remember.

We turn together to face the Followers. Behind us Rael opens the chamber door.

They blow through slowly at first, a release of white butterflies that keeps thickening until they are swarming through Star Temple. They settle on heads and shoulders, or spread their wings and flatten against the golden walls. I notice some rise as high as the ceiling. Others cluster around the windows. There must be hundreds. Thousands. The Followers start chanting, their voices soft as dust. *"Vessen terr sherrlie roomay."* Two butterflies settle in the folds of my dress. Another floats down onto the lilies that I am still clutching in my left hand.

I must not touch these butterflies. Must not even

breathe on them. They are sacred—a symbol of my Glorious Future.

But as I kneel with Howard and sway in the flow of the endless chants, I realize with a strange ache that although the release of the butterflies has been part of every Bonding I have ever watched, by the next day—the next Star Temple Meeting—there is never any trace of them.

I am still shivering. Still struggling. And I do not want to think about how the butterflies might be cleared away.

22

The Bonding ceremony took so long that it is almost dark by the time we drive up to Hill Park.

We pass the strangely shaped trees and I Image them moving on their own, their long roots tearing up from the soil as they lumber raggedly across the grounds. In my mind they are escaping, crashing out through the gates and shambling away down the drive and on beyond the farm. And then I think that this Image is some kind of madness. Why would they be escaping? It is only tiredness scratching at me.

I am to be with Howard now, for ever and always.

I have longed for this day—this night.

I feel Howard's arm around my shoulder, his leg

pressed against mine. And glancing up at him, I think that in the grey light I cannot see the wrinkles or the sallow skin. And even if I could see it, of course I should not care. The outer form is nothing and nowhere. We learn to love the soul within. We learn to love the soul within. I am lucky. So lucky. Lucky. So lucky.

We are here. Arrived.

Down the hill, by our sheds and around the farm, there are always Followers about. Always something being done. But the mansion is veiled in silence, and the windows seem to watch coldly as I stumble from the limousine.

Rael gets out from his seat at the front, and he and Howard go ahead as a Watcher steps from the shadows and helps me to the door.

"There are sixteen steps," the Watcher tells me.

I count my way carefully, but it is not easy in the beaded dress. Several times the backs of my feet catch the hem and I hear the sound of silk tearing.

"It won't matter," says the Watcher, as I struggle to lift the dragging train. "You're nearly done with it."

I am puzzled for a moment, and then realize he means the dress.

Looking ahead, I see Howard and Rael pass

through the open door, and I get a sudden flashed Image of running, racing away back down the drive and past the farm and the barns and all the fields and on into the town where all the Outsider lights are glittering and somewhere, maybe at a fair or in a Drinking Den or washed by moonlight on his Outsider bed is Jamie. Jamie. Is he thinking of me? Can he Image me as easily as I can still Image him?

"Keep going." The Watcher has his hand on my back, almost pushing me. I keep going.

The hall is wide, and darker than outside. Pale lights flicker above alcoves where ghosted statues are locked in awkward poses, as if they were turned to stone unexpectedly.

The walls between the alcoves are not flat, but sculpted with heavily painted flowers and trees. A faint light shudders as a backdrop, as if somewhere behind this scene there is a fire burning. I realize it is Endtime.

"You can leave her here, you'd better get back outside," Rael tells the Watcher, coming towards us suddenly. Then, turning to where I am standing awkwardly, his milk-pale eyes flicking across me, "Just follow Howard."

Howard is already moving on up the curving stairs. I still struggle with my dress, one hand on the heavy wooden banister. The banister is carved with vines—or snakes.

Howard has not spoken to me since we left Star Temple, the Chosen's songs still ringing as we left them behind. I wish he would. I want to get the sense of him again. I need to get back to those feelings where just a glance from him would make me tremble with an excitement I didn't quite understand. It is the Badness in me that has made everything change. I must grow beyond it. I must love Howard for ever and always. I must love him. I must love him. I must love him.

The top of the stairs opens into a long corridor. There are rooms and rooms and rooms, but all the doors are shut. I am not sure how many Brides there should be. Much of the past is still misted. But I am sure there has been one new Bonding for every year since I was Chosen, and the Divine Writings had ordered Howard to choose his Brides five years before that, so there must be fifteen.

We pass more alcoves with the awkward statues. The walls are still painted with Endtime paradise and I can see in the spill of gaslight that the paints are oils, and the walls have the grain of an artist's canvas.

We have reached what must be the back of the

house, for there is an arched window with more creeping shapes coiling round its frame. A cold moon stares in through the glass, throwing a silver glance on another of the statues. It shocks me, the statue, for I realize suddenly it is not human. Not quite. None of them are.

Their eyes are too slanted. Their limbs too angular—and wire thin. Every forehead is marked with the True Cause W and I realize they must be Beings beyond Endtime. Images from Howard's Flash of the Future. The children of the Brides.

I am trying not to cry. I am lucky, so lucky, to be Chosen for all of this. Except I cannot feel it. I cannot feel that luck has brought me here.

Bad Thoughts. Bad Thoughts.

There is a door to the right and Howard's dry-leaf hand grips the handle. The door swings open soundlessly.

This new room is white. White walls. White carpet.

And in the centre, a huge white bed.

I suddenly do not want to step inside this room. I do not want the door to swing shut behind me.

The room is not lit, and the whiteness gives off a hushed glow that makes me suddenly remember watching a fox in the snow. I am being held by a window, and I am in the arms of Maria. My mother. *Think for yourself, Maria. Think for yourself.* The fox was so magical, its body gold against the frozen night. It stood rigid, scenting the air, its ears laid back and listening. And then it ran. The next morning I found its trail scudding across the centre of our garden. Our garden. I have never remembered our garden before.

Howard turns to me. Comes to me. I stand fox-still as he rips apart the ties at the back of the beaded dress, tearing it from my shoulders.

I am pressed backwards onto the bed and I have never lain anywhere so soft. Or so terrible.

I must love Howard. I must love him. I must love him. But I am numb.

The dress is wrenched down over my hips and legs. I do nothing to help. My head knows what is happening, but my body does not feel it. He pulls at my underclothes and then he is on me, rough and fumbling, his breath in my face.

I do not move. Do not make a sound.

My hands stay locked to my sides and I stay staring up over his shoulder and past his left ear while he buries himself in me with hard ugly grunts that make me think of pigs in pain.

I must love him. I must love him.

He stops suddenly, and withdraws from me. I hear a rustle and crunch and realize he must be standing on the beaded dress.

I still do not move, not even when I hear the door swing open, his footsteps walking away down the long corridor.

Is that it? Is that really it?

My eyes stay fixed on the ceiling and I can see, even in the dark, that there are cracks everywhere.

23

"Happy morning. I'm Bronwyn—Howard's first Bride—and I've come to prepare you for the day."

I sit up slowly, surprised to discover I have climbed inside the sheets and slept. The Bride called Bronwyn is walking towards me. She is dressed in white, a flimsy white that is almost transparent in the morning light, and she smiles at me with eyes alight with love.

"Your cleansing room is through that door." Bronwyn stands by the end of the big white bed and I notice for the first time another door in the corner of the room. And other things too. A white cupboard and a white chest. White flowers in slim white vases. A wide window behind heavy white curtains.

"You cleanse in a bath. You might find it a bit strange at first, but it's very exotic."

"Isn't there a cleansing spray?" There are no baths down at the farm.

"Howard wishes us to be submerged every morning, because it softens the soul. There will be lots of new things that you haven't done before, but I'm here to help you. All of us are."

Bronwyn goes to the cupboard and opens the door. There is a rail of white dresses and shawls, and underneath a rack of strappy-heeled shoes. "Put this on." She chooses me a white satin robe. "I'll run your water while you get up."

I pull on the robe that barely reaches my thighs. I am aching all over, as if I have been climbing hills.

Walking unsteadily and cringing from the muffled warmth of the carpet, my bare foot crunches something small and hard. I squint down and see a crystal bead. Just one. The dress is gone. I pick it up and it glistens like a teardrop on my palm. "Someone must have come in the night. Taken the dress," I call shakily. Did Howard come back? I realize that I am troubled by the idea of this. But it is a Bad Thought. Last night was the beginning of my Glorious Future. I have wanted it. Longed for it. I do not understand why I feel so unclean.

I hear the sound of running water, and Bronwyn comes back out and hugs me. "You don't need to worry about anything here. Everything is taken care of. You just have to be happy. That's what Howard wants for us all."

A haze of steam clouds up from behind the white door.

Bronwyn fetches a fluffy white towel, and hands it to me. "We are lucky here. So lucky." She smiles.

"Lucky. So lucky." I take the towel and force myself to enter the room of clouds. The heat suffocates me. The water has foamed into a mountain of bubbles. "What do I do?" I ask.

"Just enjoy it. There are perfumes and oils that will soak to your soul. All Brides are pure. All Brides are clear."

I go to step into the water, and Bronwyn laughs suddenly. It is an odd sound. Unexpected—even in someone who is happy. So happy. "You need to take the robe off," she giggles.

24

This room is all glass. I sit with the other Brides at the long crystal table which is laid out with fruited rice dishes and jugs of lemon water.

There are trees inside this room—real trees—not artificial ones. And flowers and ferns and bushes and vines.

There are birds, too, caged in miniature golden Star Temples that hang from the branches of the trees. The birds are white, and their singing is a rich background against the murmuring of the Brides.

Bronwyn offers me one of the dishes, and I empty it clumsily onto my plate. A scatter of rice and sliced strawberry spills down onto my lap. Two other Brides help me clean it up quickly, but not before a red smear has stained my white dress. "I'm surprised the birds sing." I say this because I feel awkward and want to move the attention away, but once the words are out I grow strangely giddy, as if I am looking down over the edge of something.

The murmuring stops, and fifteen pale china-doll faces turn to me.

"All birds sing, don't they?" Katrina, a bride whom I almost recognize, is looking as if I have said I am surprised birds can compose music.

"But in cages." I stir my food slowly, as if mixing it together is the most important thing in the world. I am remembering that other long-ago strawberry. And Meryl. "I would have thought birds hate being in cages."

The bird song becomes shriller against the long silence.

"That's a strange idea." Another bride—I think she is called Anna but there are so many names—spears a slice of orange with her fork and offers it to Katrina. "The birds have a perfect life. They never have to worry about cats or hawks or anything dangerous."

"And they'd never survive outside. They wouldn't know how to." Katrina stretches her neck and takes the sliced orange with her teeth, at the same time offering back a black grape on her own fork.

"They're lucky. So lucky." The bride who may be Anna nods her head at everyone.

"Lucky. So lucky," they all say.

The murmuring starts up again.

I put my fork down and look out across the grounds. I am seeing a view from the back of the mansion—not visible from the drive—and it fascinates me to think that this has always been here, and I have not known. There is a path leading away from our indoor garden, running down to a lake. Water dances out of a fountain in the middle, and narrowing my eyes I can see a rainbow caught in the spray. There are statues that line the path and the edges of the lake, as strange and awkward as the ones in the corridors. Some of the bushes and trees are heavy with white blossom, and the slow drift of petals makes me think of butterflies.

"There are fish in that lake." Bronwyn smiles and nods at me eagerly. "Really big ones."

"Silver," says Katrina, opening her hands wide to show me the size. "As big as a baby."

I shiver suddenly. Fish. Baby. Fish. Baby. Another memory I do not want.

"The statues," I say suddenly, needing to fill my head with something else, "they all look so unusual . . ."

The murmuring stops again, and this time I realize I am standing at an edge with a sharper drop.

My hands are shaking slightly as I look down at them. Take care. Take care. "The statues seem very special."

"They are." Bronwyn smiles. "Very special."

"Very special." The others nod and smile with her as though their heads are connected in some way. Maybe they are. Maybe they have reached a higher level of Prediction Practice and even their movements are completely in tune. Is that what will happen to me?

I sip the lemon water, and as soon as it is finished Katrina pours me a fresh glass. I take it although I am bloated out with water and fruited rice. I would like to lie down, although not in the luxury bed. I would like to be curled tight in my bunk.

Bronwyn takes my hand and strokes the back of it with her pale thin fingers. "We're so happy that you were called," she says.

"I'm so happy too." I watch her fingers lace mine. She does seem happy. They all seem happy. We are lucky. So lucky.

The trill of the birds is suddenly overwhelming.

Outside the sky has a hint of blue. I think about how it must be having a hint of blue over Jamie too.

A Watcher drives past on a mowing machine, and a whirl of cut grass spins a mad dance behind him.

I think about how Howard can hear the grass grow. I wonder what sort of noise it is making now.

25

Bronwyn has her arm through mine and she guides me up a curving staircase and along a blackened corridor. We have reached another floor and I think we must somehow be in the roof of the house. The tiny gaslights that are set near the ceiling throw down thin beams that cross each other as they fall.

"This is the place—it's very special in here." We stand opposite a door, and Bronwyn squeezes my hand. "You are here for Enlightenment. After today the new truth will rise up in you and it will be golden and glorious."

Golden and glorious. I Image the words in my mind and they stretch and grow, like flames.

Bronwyn opens the door and nudges me forward. I am in a room that is blacker than the corridor. The dark swells like a creature contained in a space too small, its sides pressing at the walls. I wonder what shape this dark would take if it was released. Or perhaps it would not take any shape—but would just keep pouring and spreading out into the daylight. Filling the world.

Think for yourself, Maria. Think for yourself.

I struggle against this sudden memory of my mother, but it pushes back at me. It is night time and I am in a different room—in a bed with her. I am curled against her back and although it is dark I do not mind that she is asleep, because the steady rhythm of her breathing is enough.

Then the Image slides and I am back in the present again. Back in the dark, dark room. I become aware that something is happening. Pinpricks of light spark out from what I realize is a domed ceiling. I am staring up at a sky full of stars.

"Pretty, isn't it?"

This is a man's voice, and as he speaks two torches on pillars begin to flame on either side of him. The domed ceiling washes from black to grey to dusky gold, and the stars burn away. Except one. One star is left, diamond bright in the centre of the dome. I turn towards the man's voice, and see Rael spinning round to face me from a black chair that swivels. He is all dressed in black, too—black boots and trousers and a black high-necked jumper.

"Sit." He points to an identical chair opposite.

I sit awkwardly, uncomfortable with the idea of a chair that moves. I press my bare feet hard on the black tiled floor, afraid that I may start swinging about without any control.

Rael is smiling, the room now flickering gold. I have never seen Rael smile before.

I press my feet down harder, just focusing on keeping still. There are no windows and the flamed pillars give off a faint waft of gas. It is pressingly hot, and I feel a sense of danger in this airless place.

"It's good that you're with us." The smile twists slightly. "Good you've been Called."

"I'm happy that it's happened at last," I say.

"It's important that you listen properly today—before I can let you leave this special place I will need to see that you understand." Rael leans back in his chair as if he is relaxing, but his eyes stay fixed on my face as he drops his voice. "Have you ever thought about how True Cause began?"

I can answer this. I have heard it enough times. "It began as a vision. Although it was not just a vision . . ."

He cuts across my chant. "But before the vision. What about before the vision?"

I try to think. I see the mound that is my mother asleep in the warm dark room. Are these the sorts of thing he wants to know? I do not think so. Take care. Take care. "Howard is our True Cause Master. I don't know what there can have been before him."

"Did you exist? Did anyone exist?"

Another scene seeps out from my memory. A parcel. The paper is brightly patterned. Balloons, I think. When I tear at the paper I see a soft brown ear. A soft brown paw. I feel a thrill for a moment—almost as if it is happening now—and then remember Rael. "Without Howard Our Master, I'm sure we were nothing," I say.

"How can that be? Someone must have put Howard at the bottom of that hill. Something must have brought him that vision."

I try thinking this through, but nothing will come. Only the bear. He had warm honey eyes and a blue silk ribbon round his neck. "I . . . I don't know. Was it someone more powerful than Howard?"

"There's no one more powerful than Howard. Howard is Master of all things."

"Howard is Master of all things."

"And more too, Elinor. So much more." Rael

leans closer. "Howard is the *cosmic* Master. He has evolved from beyond."

I nod, although I am not clear what he means.

"Once you are Enlightened we can't let you Outside again—but you'll have moved to a higher level of True Cause understanding. This is Howard's gift to you—and to all of his Chosen. You are lucky." He pauses, his voice dropping to a whisper. "Tell me what you are."

"I am lucky. So lucky."

When I was sad I used to bury my face in the bear's soft fur.

"Are you ready for Enlightenment?"

"I am ready for Enlightenment."

I remember I called the bear Gruffles.

The room is darkening again, slipping back through gold and grey. "Just watch the star, Elinor. Keep looking at it."

The one star blinks down from the domed ceiling like the hard bright eye of a bird.

"A long time ago—many thousands of years—there was the planet Ecutaruse. The beings of Ecutaruse were a slender, pale-skinned race with silver-white hair and eyes darker than darkness. They were an advanced race who practised Prediction and Sudden Sight. If they'd survived, their knowledge and wisdom would by now have been so great, they'd have been masters of the universe. But they didn't. Their planet was doomed. For all their great wisdom, they couldn't stop the giant meteorite that smashed into Ecutaruse, destroying everything."

As Rael speaks, a streak of gold flashes across the dome and crashes against the one star. They wrestle above me, then fragments explode outwards in a spray of gold and silver lights.

"Howard's Divine Writings have revealed all this. The Divine Writings are showing us the way."

"The Divine Writings are showing us the way." I am trying—really trying—to listen but I am remembering that I had a music box too. It was black and decorated with glittery jewels. A tiny ballerina spun round when the lid was lifted, although I was never allowed to lift the lid on my own.

Above me, the battle of the stars is fading. Only the tiniest flicker still winks and blinks. I must keep my focus on it. I must concentrate. Concentrate.

"Except—it wasn't all hopeless. The Ecutaruse lords, aware of impending doom, gathered their Highest Order males in a special, secret building. With the building sealed tight against outside distractions, the chosen members entered a Trance of Transcendence. In this transcended state they were able to leave Ecutaruse and travel through space. Their task was to populate a new planet by bonding with whatever existing life forms they discovered."

I become aware of a small red light that flashes on and off, on and off, moving out from the explosion.

"Some of those chosen Ecutarusians found Earth!" The red light hovers, then blinks off. Rael's voice hisses, "Still look at the star, Elinor. Look at the star."

I look at the star.

"The chosen of Ecutaruse mated with the daughters of early humans, and the fruit of these daughters came out looking part Ecutaruse and part human. But the true Ecutarusians didn't survive long on Earth. The Writings tell us that the necessary intensity of the Trance of Transcendence had weakened them. They didn't die in any normal way, but their bodies slowly crumbled to dust. It's this dust that marks your forehead in the Bonding ceremony. The Dust of Destiny. Are you still listening? Do you understand?"

I nod and touch my forehead, but I have Imaged a new picture now. It was a boy who gave me Gruffles. He used to come to our house and play, and he came with a man who had a beard. Me and Gruffles. Our house. Our house. I am remembering rooms in our Outsider house.

Rael's voice shadows the Image. "But still, in the space of time they had, the Ecutaruse Chosen achieved well. They left behind their legacy of pale-haired, black-eyed, half-Ecutarusian offspring. These children, in their turn, bonded with normal humans and new children were born of these Bondings. In this way the line has kept going, although of course it's in a diluted form."

My room was yellow, the colour of primroses. The dancing ballerina box was on a shelf above my bed. And there was a rocking horse and a doll's house and . . .

"Except for one child—Wordah. It is believed Wordah was the only child to be the union of two Ecutarusian parents on Earth—a female had hidden in the secret building, and she entered the Trance of Transcendence with the other males. Her story is in the Divine Writings. You may read her gospel one day."

. . . I used to like reading. I remember fairies and dogs and giants and . . .

"So Wordah was a true Ecutarusian. The last. And he was deeply impressive, even by the elevated Ecutaruse standards. Right from an early age he predicted that at some point in the future, Endtime would come upon Earth, as it had come to his own planet. He wanted to develop Beings who would evolve beyond this. He wanted to save as many as he could. He saw it as his mission—his reason for being."

We left our house at night. A van came for us. I remember my mother carrying me to it and telling me it would be all right from now on. We would not be struggling on our own against evil anymore. I had not understood her, because we were not on our own. We had each other. And Gruffles. Except I had to leave Gruffles behind. Possessions weigh down the soul.

"Wordah trained his mind beyond even the most powerful of the Ecutaruse Masters . . ."

I hated the rice so much at first. And all the sitting still in the Meetings. And after each Meeting my mother became more distant from me, and she never talked about anything except True Cause.

Rael's voice is soft and low now. "When Wordah reached sixteen he bonded with a human. To his joy and delight the union created a child, and the child was both gifted and strong. It is from this child that Howard's line evolved. Howard is a direct descendant of Wordah, and that's why he's our Master. He is finishing the job for Wordah. For Ecutarusians.

"Beyond Endtime, there's a New Age coming. This is written. This is known. Howard's holding back from wasting his seed now, but after the Day of Destruction it will be the honour of the Brides to bear his fruit. Your young will grow and Bond with each other, and in time seed the new Master Race. You are lucky, so lucky."

"I am lucky, so lucky."

Rael leans back in his chair. "You have heard it now. Enlightenment. Our beginnings. Are you moved by this, Elinor? Are you Elevated?"

My eyes are aching as I stare up at the star that is no longer there. I want to be happy about seeding the new Master Race. I want to Image this Glorious Future, but somehow it doesn't seem real. What seems real is this more private truth. My mother. My own beginnings.

I realize Rael is watching me and his eyes are slitted. I am not pleasing him.

It is hot in this room. Burning hot. I feel slightly sick with the smell of gas and I pass my hand across my forehead, looking towards the torches. The flames diminish on them until they are just tiny flickers, and Rael is watching me closely. I have a faint idea that he is controlling them somehow, and I am uneasy with this idea of his power, but I dare not show it. "The truth is Golden and Glorious," I say, dazzling him with my Spread-the-Word smile. "I am lucky. So lucky."

26

I am dreaming that I am much much younger. It is raining, and I am in Braxbury with my mother, and an older Follower who has hardly looked at me. She has not even asked me my name. We are standing at the corner of the street and my mother and the older Follower are thrusting The Book at Outsiders who are passing by. "Have you ever wondered why we're here . . . ?" The passersby are not showing any level of response, but I am wondering why we are here. It is miserably cold. I tug at my mother's shawl but she takes no notice.

"Have you ever wondered why we're here? Have you ever wondered why we're here?"

An Outsider comes up to talk to the older Follower.

This Outsider does show a Positive Response because he keeps flicking through The Book, nodding and turning the pages.

My mother steps back from them both slightly, as if she senses that the Outsider needs some space to help him take in the information.

She throws her attention at other passing Outsiders. "Have you ever wondered why we're here? Have you ever wondered why we're here?"

And suddenly there is a car beside us and a man—a man with a beard—is wedging himself between my mother and the other Follower, pushing her into the car. Pushing us both in.

The bearded man climbs into the back of the car, and I am squashed in the middle against him and my mother.

For a moment the older Follower tries to get at us, banging on the window and grappling with the door handle on my mother's side. My mother is shouting and banging back, but the driver—a man with a shock of ginger hair—speeds us off with a squeal of tyres.

"True Cause is the true cause. True Cause is the true cause. Leave us alone. You have no right . . ." My mother is still thumping on the door, her hands reaching out to the older Follower who is slipping into the distance.

I think that, if the door suddenly opened, my mother would leap away out of the speeding car and roll into the road.

I am scared, but, glancing sideways, I see the face of the bearded man, and although he looks anxious, it is not him who frightens me. It is not the ginger man either—even though he is driving so fast.

It is my mother who scares me, with her wide blank stare and her droning chant. "True Cause is the true cause. True Cause is the true cause."

"I don't want to be with True Cause, Mummy. I want to be back at home." She keeps on chanting and takes no notice of me. But I keep whispering it anyway.

27

The dream is still with me when I wake. I am sure the other Brides do not dream like this. I am sure there is something very wrong with me, but I am scared to Unburden because they are such Bad Thoughts. Bad Thoughts.

"Happy morning." Bronwyn smiles at me as I enter the glass room for breakfast.

"Happy morning."

"Happy morning."

"I love you."

"I love you."

The Brides hand round the dishes of fruit, and pour the sweetened water. Their voices are a background haze, their smiles so bright and blank. I long to blend in with them. Lose myself. Be lulled by the True Cause warmth that seems to wrap around them like a blanket. It seems so easy. And so safe. Except that I cannot quite do it. Something in me is always holding back.

I am held back from Howard too.

He comes to me most nights and each time I lie statue still, staring at the ceiling, hearing his pig-harsh grunts and smelling his breath in my face.

And, although I try to block the Image away, I keep remembering how different it felt to be touched by Jamie.

"Do you want some crystallized apple?" Helena leans across and passes the plate to me.

I take a piece and chew it slowly, but it tastes dead and dry.

I think about the skin on Howard's hands.

28

"Howard wants you. The Washing of the Feet."

I turn from the window of my white room, where I have been watching Rael's black Mercedes slide away down the drive, and stare at Bronwyn. "The Washing of the Feet?"

"It is a great privilege. You are lucky. So lucky."

"Lucky. So lucky." I walk with her through a part of the mansion that is new to me. I think I have been here for several weeks, but the size of the place is still a mystery. And there is a whole wing that has been Forbidden. Until now. There is not much difference—the same paintings and statues. Winding stairs. Long thin corridors. Occasional glimpses of the grounds, and the farm and fields beyond. The sky today is a hazed blue.

A wisped memory floats up of Imogen and Felicity. I will see them again when it is their turn to be Called, and for a moment I am filled with warmth at the thought of it. Although it is getting harder to Image their faces.

At one point I notice double doors up in front of us, and the door is modern, not heavy wood with carvings like the rest. I think that this must be where we are headed, but Bronwyn hurries on, leaving me to startle backwards over my shoulder at a sudden but distinctive sound. It is the same sound Jamie's mobile telephone made when it rang in the woods that day. As I think of this, I think of him. See his face. Moss-green eyes. The way he smiled. It hurts when he comes to me like this. Why can I Image him, and not the other Chosen? Bad Thoughts. Bad Thoughts. Maybe I deserve this pain, and will never be properly free.

The door that we finally stop at is embossed gold. I think, as Bronwyn knocks twice, that I should have expected this. What else would Howard choose?

"Just leave when you're finished. I'll be waiting to lead you back." She hugs me. "I love you. Be happy."

"I love you too."

Howard is seated in a chair of white leather. He is not robed, but is instead in gold silk trousers and a gold silk jacket with wide quilted shoulders. The shoulders make me think of wings. His feet, I notice, are bare.

He raises a goblet of gold liquid to me, in the Outsider gesture that I remember Jamie made with his pint of toxic beer. Behind me the door has closed.

For a long moment nothing happens. Then he says, "Go through to the Cleansing Room. Bronwyn has already prepared the bowl. Just bring it through."

I keep my eyes lowered, but I know he is watching me as I move past him. He does not seem angry, but I remember how quickly he can flare up. Why can I not open up to Howard like I did to Jamie? Maybe I should Unburden to Bronwyn about what to do. How to be.

I walk slowly into the tiled room, the mosaic floor and domed ceiling making it like a miniature Star Temple. There is a gold hand basin and a gold bath, and in the bath there is a golden bowl shining with silver rainbow suds.

I lift the bowl carefully, but I am suddenly shaking and the suds slosh out onto my hands where they blink at me as if they are sharing secrets.

Back in the main room Howard has leant back in the leather seat, his legs stretched in front of him on what I see now is a white bear rug. There is a bottle of the gold liquid on a small gold table.

"Come to me. And kneel," he commands.

Still sloshing I carry the bowl and lower it down. The head of the bear rolls slightly, as if it is irritated that I have disturbed it. It has black glass eyes and its mouth is wrinkled back in an angry snarl. Its teeth look real.

"Roll up my trousers."

Kneeling before Howard, I turn the bottom of his trousers up. It is a struggle because they are so tight and I have to touch his bare skin and touching his bare skin freezes something in the centre of me. I would like to jolt away from him, but on the outside, at least, I must stay calm and blank. I must not risk his anger. His legs are coarse with wiry gold hair, and his feet too. He lifts one of the feet and I take it—concentrate, concentrate—and place it in the bowl.

I can feel him watching me, and hear the small swallows of sound he makes as he sips from his goblet. His voice has a lazy edge when he speaks. "You are harder to reach than any of the others, Elinor. I have observed this in you."

I concentrate—concentrate—swishing the suds

which have caught all the golds of the room. The whole bowl glimmers like liquid treasure.

I feel his hand touch my shoulder, stroke my hair.

Concentrate. Concentrate. I am lucky. So lucky.

He lifts his foot suddenly, suds frothing down onto the white bear, and a moment later the other foot is in. "Just massage it. Be especially firm around the ankles, and between the toes." He sighs slowly, leaning forward to caress the back of my neck. "Some days I ache and ache."

I try to pretend that his foot is just a lump of wood. It is only dead bark that I am touching. But it is too soft for wood and his toenails scrape my fingers and it takes everything I have not to jerk away.

I sat on dead wood with Jamie. He stroked my hair. It felt beautiful.

"It is right that you don't follow blindly," Howard says suddenly. I am not sure what he is telling me and think it is best not to answer. It seems, anyway, that there is no need for me to reply because he pours himself more gold liquid, and goes on, "It hasn't been easy for me either. I battled against everything in the beginning."

He lifts his foot from the bowl and I glance up, startled, thinking that he has guessed what I am feeling. He is gifted with Sudden Sight. He has evolved through a direct line from Wordah. He must surely know everything. Everything. But he is clever, of course. He is masking it well. I look up at him cautiously and see that he is staring past me, looking towards the gold-curtained window where the hazed blue sky is still pouring in.

"I was so troubled," he says. "Voices talked to me in a language I could not understand. Beings visited me in my room at night. They told me—Enlightened me—about who I was—why I was here. But I struggled to believe it, Elinor. I did not want it."

I shift slightly and the bear head twists again and one eye seems to fix me with an angry glare. My knees are numbing up. I wonder again if I am expected to speak.

"I thought I was losing my mind at first." Howard laughs—the sound eerily high. Tipping back more of the gold liquid he gulps heavily, then reaches for the bottle again. "I wanted to be normal, Elinor. Just an ordinary Outsider. Can you under-stand how that feels?"

"Yes." I remember my whisperings in the dream. *I don't want to be with True Cause, Mummy. I want to be back at home.*

"I knew you would, because I see the struggle in

you, too, and through you I see myself as I was then—not so much older. You probably do not think of that, do you—you probably cannot Image me so young."

"I . . ." I am saved from answering because he is hurrying on.

"I was at university, studying drama. I had no family—I never knew my part-Ecutarusian father, who left home because he was lost and confused about who he was. This is not uncommon—or even surprising—for anyone who had not been Enlightened about their Wordah lineage. My mother—who was not of the line, of course—died a few years later. I was brought up in foster homes, and never truly happy. But when I reached university I wanted to put all those sorrows behind me, and was ready to look ahead. But I was badly used—I didn't 'fit' and the tutors blocked me from getting a few top roles that should have been mine. I was devastated."

He is gulping the gold liquid now as if it will evaporate if he does not finish it quickly.

"I had Imaged such a Glorious Future on the stage, but without support I began to doubt myself. Of course, I know now that all of this was as it should be—the cosmos was working to reveal my true path to me. It does that for all of us, if we can learn to trust. Do you trust, Elinor?"

"I trust. I trust." I suppose the energy of the cosmos has even played its part in this washing of the feet, although I do not say this.

"Rael wasn't at university, but this time fate brought us together through the sharing of accommodation. He sold insurance, but his employer was a low-grade company that manipulated and deceived its customers. Eventually the management abused him, making out he had stolen company money. It was a difficult time for him. You'd hardly think he'd have time for me and my distress, but he did . . ." His voice becomes distant, as if this Imaging is painful. ". . . in the end, it was Rael that saw the truth of what was happening to me. If it hadn't been for Rael . . ."

He stops talking and I look up at him, trying honestly to picture him and Rael as young as me. Or as young as Jamie. Once Howard and Rael were as young as Jamie. "What did Rael do?" I suddenly need to know, and for some reason with his words slurring and his eyes slightly hazed I am less afraid of Howard than I have ever been.

"He guided me. Supported me. He helped me to understand that what was happening was not madness, which was one of my tormented beliefs, but a Greater Truth. I owe so much to Rael. Without him, I may never have found the Path. And without finding the Path, where would we all be . . ." He lifts his goblet in the Jamie gesture, and tries to drink from it again. The goblet does not quite connect with his mouth and a thin line of the liquid dribbles down his chin. "True Cause is the true cause," he is half chanting, half singing. "True Cause is the true cause."

"True Cause is the true cause. True Cause is the true cause," I reply.

Suddenly he grips my shoulders, pinching the skin through my thin white shift. "Tell me you believe, Elinor. Let me hear you say it."

I stare at him in panic. I relaxed my fear of him, and inside that moment he saw some terrible truth in me. "I believe. I believe," I say hurriedly.

He shakes his head. "You are so like me. You have never quite fitted. I have sensed it on you. Smelt it on you." There is a light in his eyes now, more like the burning gaze of the Howard who stands in Star Temple.

Maybe I should Unburden to him. Take the risk. He has probably caught my thoughts anyway, so there is nothing to lose. "I have struggled sometimes. I'm sorry. So sorry."

I wait for him to draw more from me, but I am puzzled as his eyes fill with tears. He lifts my hair, sieving it through his fingers. "I knew you were special.

The Chosen of the Chosen. The most Blessed of all the Brides. Beyond Endtime it will be your fruit that is the ripest. Your fruit and mine. By this hair and those eyes I have known you, and been waiting. Waiting."

I try to smile but my mouth feels stiff and I lower my eyes, uncertain what to do or say. The liquid treasure has all gone now, leaving only a scum of white on the surface of the water.

"There is not much time. The Divine Writings are showing me this." Howard's voice is suddenly urgent. "But whatever happens, we will be together. You and me. The Chosen of the Chosen."

"You and me, the Chosen of the Chosen," I try to whisper back, but the reply dies in my throat and I cannot say it. Cannot feel it.

But anyway I do not think he has noticed because he is leaning away, his head drooping sideways and his eyes closed.

Very quietly I get up and carry the water back into the cleansing room, tipping it away into the hand basin and hoping that its tired gurgle does not wake him again.

Bronwyn is outside, exactly as she promised she would be. She hugs me. "It is a special thing, the Washing of the Feet. Whenever I have done it I feel very close to Howard. And my head is always full of such beautiful things."

I nod and smile. "I feel that too," I say. But I am remembering that time with the Prediction Practice Counsellor, when I was Imaging strawberries that he did not see. And just now, with Howard, I wanted to Unburden, but he could not catch my need. I did not feel close to him at all. I feel messed up and muddled and my head is full of Jamie again.

29

The High Order Followers who prepare all our food have gone back Downstairs, leaving the long table with its snow-white cloth set for two. Light dances up off the gold cutlery that is laid at either end, and there are napkins folded into the shapes of birds and butterflies.

The room has the scent of bread, and there are plates of pineapple and passion fruit, red and yellow peppers in an oil-gold sauce, salad arranged like a garden of flowers, cheeses and cherries and gold-crusted pies with the True Cause star decorating the lids.

From the centre of the table there rises a small golden statue, its head thrown back and its arms reaching to the ceiling. I have seen Howard stand like that. Often. I am waiting with the other Brides, all of us lining the walls as we do every afternoon at this time. The star-patterned mosaic floor is cold on my feet.

"They are getting closer. This morning I was struck by Sudden Sight, and I could sense the danger." The door opens and Howard strides in, followed by Rael. "They're trying to crush me. To kill my flame. But nothing and no one will put out the light that burns in me. And we'll find a way to stop their demon lies. I don't care what we do—the end will justify the means."

He sits at the head of the table, and Rael takes his place at the other end. We move forward, all of us Brides in one go, and begin passing them the food. They both take as much as they can fit on their plates.

Howard seems distracted today. He takes up a gold-crusted pie, but his hand starts shaking as he holds it to his lips. He drops it back to his plate. "I need to write," he mutters. "There are messages coming through."

Bronwyn hurries forward and hastily removes his plate, and Rael gets up and goes to a heavily carved chest beneath the window.

The book he brings out has a white leather cover with True Cause writing embossed across it. There is a pen too. Golden. It rests on a white silk cushion. Martha takes the book and Mary takes the cushion, both carrying them across the room to Howard. He waves his hand at the table of food. "Take this away." He sounds as if he is close to shouting. Or screaming. "The smell of it is clogging up the Channels."

The Followers reappear. There is the chink of china as they scurry backwards and forwards, loading everything onto an ornate white trolley.

As the table is cleared Howard aims his focus on the golden statue. His eyes become strange and distant, and he sways.

It surprises me how quickly everything is hurried away, and I think that the Followers must have done this before. Probably many times. But although I have a brief question in my mind about where all the food goes, I am too engaged in what is about to happen to stay with the thought for long. I have not seen this before—the act of Divine Writing—and I am honoured that I am the Bride standing closest to Howard. I will be able to see how it happens.

A long time passes.

I am aware of my breathing. I try to stand statue still, but my legs are aching and it is uncomfortable.

And then at last Howard picks up the pen and begins to write. His hand moves quickly now, his head shaking. Sometimes he smacks his fist onto the table. There are beads of sweat on his forehead and he is murmuring all the time, using True Cause words but I know they are of the Advanced Level because I can only pick out some that I understand.

Rael understands though, and with every muttering he nods and sends Howard Advanced Level answers back.

Howard shouts. I jump, looking round at the other Brides. Not one of them has even flinched. And Howard is lost in the Writings again.

There are strange things happening to him now. I can see a violent twitch in his cheek and his hands. His legs begin to flail about, jerking outwards unexpectedly. But he is still writing, the words swirling out from the nib of the pen in a wild unstoppable flow.

Glancing sideways at Rael I see he has made a tent with his fingers and is leaning forward with his chin on the tip, just watching.

Suddenly with a scream Howard falls sideways, clutching at the edge of the tablecloth. The gold pen spins away across the floor and the book slides with the cloth and drops down next to where Howard is lying, his whole body shuddering.

"Your Master is receiving Cosmic Rejuvenation." I realize my eyes must be boggling and that Rael is talking to me. "When he is returned to us he will be stronger and even more powerful. You may retrieve the book."

I step forward, trembling partly because of the scene I have just witnessed, and partly because I am sure that to be this close to Divine Writings is a wonderful thing. A glorious thing.

I try not to look at Howard, terrified that if I do I may affect the process in some way. I pick up the book and some of the pages have been bent awkwardly with the fall. The fact that they may be creased seems terrible to me, so I open the covers to smooth them flat.

"Don't do that!" Rael's voice is like a slap. "Just bring it to me."

I hurry over to him, frightened by his tone, and by the added fear that he may know what I have seen.

I could not help the glimpse I had. A glimpse of one waved line repeated over and over across the pages, an endless *WWWWWWWWWWWWWWW*. Howard has not written any words at all.

30

I am in my white room, and I am staring out of the window towards the lake. I see rippling and I think about Howard's silver fish all sliding beneath the skin of the water. And then I Image baby Bella and Caroline Markham. And Isabel with her reeded hair as they carried her away. I squint up my eyes but although I can make out the tree where they tied Meryl, I cannot see if the bands are still there. But it does not matter. There are things that I know I will never quite Erase.

Things that troubled me. Shadows beneath my skin.

And now a new knowledge is sliding upwards. I cannot see it yet. It is only ripples. But it is waiting.

"I wondered where you were."

I flip round to see Bronwyn standing, smiling.

I want to test her. Push at her. "The Divine Writings," I say suddenly. "Have you ever looked in the book?"

"We must trust in Howard. Trust True Cause." Beneath the smile her face is blank and bland. How many layers are there covering her up? How much has she really forgotten?

She comes forward and takes my hand and I let my fingers stay hooked by her grip. It is not a strong hold. I could easily pull my hand away. But I stay there facing her and I look and look into her eyes, as if by looking long enough I will finally see through to the depths of her.

She keeps smiling back at me. There is nothing to see.

And suddenly the knowledge breaks out in a gasp for air—not from her but from me. I have not understood everything, but I can understand enough.

The writing. Howard's Divine Writing. These are the words that have shaped True Cause. They have laid down our rules. Given us our purpose. We have sold these words in the streets. We have hung our hopes on every new sentence. We have lived our lives by them. We would have died for them.

And they are not real words. Just books and books and books of *WWWW* . . .

And if they are not real, then True Cause cannot be real. It is just some game or some trick or some terrible deceit.

A way for Howard to get rich, conning New Joiners into giving up their possessions for him. Conning all of us to work work work for True Cause.

As I think this, I suddenly remember Jamie's last words to me:

"*. . . And if it all starts to make sense—proper Outsider sense I mean—then ring me.*"

31

I am scared. I should not be here.

I have been creeping and sneaking, freezing if the floor creaks. Breathing too hard. Howard is out. Rael will be with him. Howard never goes Outside without Rael, and I have checked for the car from my white room window.

But there are no windows along this corridor to check if they've come back.

I may not have long, but I am at the door. The door to the room where I heard the ringing of the telephone. My heart is thumping and my mouth is dry.

Howard could be waiting here. Or Rael. They could have caught my thoughts, or received

Sudden Sight. But I do not think so. I have stopped believing they can do anything like that.

I push on the handle, and I am in. The room seems empty. Feels empty. There is no heart but mine thump thump thumping in here.

It is all black and chrome. A leather chair. Smoked-glass tables and silver cabinets. Shelves and shelves of Outsider books. The books are the sorts of things we always had to burn after the New Joiner clearings. I skim the titles. *The Power of Persuasion. The Mind of Man. Trance and Trauma.* I would like to take them down and look at them but there is not much time. There is not much time.

I notice a desk in one corner. A silver cabinet is pressed up next to it. I slink around the edge of the room, my eyes scanning for a telephone. I am not quite sure where it will be kept—or even how to use it if I find it—and one bit of me thinks I can only hope to hear his voice. Let him hear mine. But another bit—a bit I am trying not to cling to—is Imaging that he will find a way to come for me, bundle me into a car like the bearded man bundled my mother.

There are drawers on the desk. I try them but they are locked. On the top of the cabinet is a crystal jar with a glass stopper, filled with more of the gold liquid. Still no telephone.

Perhaps I only Imaged that ringing sound. Or dreamt it. I am getting good at dreaming. Too good.

A sudden sound jolts me.

A crunch of tyres on the gravel outside.

My throat is dry and my heart is like a trapped bird as I edge to the window and look out. It is just a Watcher arriving on the mowing machine. A false alarm. There is not much time. There is not much time.

I cannot think where else to look, so I edge back to the cabinet. I am getting desperate. The cabinet has a thin chrome handle and I pull it hard, certain it will be locked but thinking that perhaps I can surprise it open—jerk it at an odd angle or something. Except the cabinet surprises me. The door opens easily and I am peering inside at a stack of Outsider newspapers.

I run my hand down the outside of the stack, and am stunned by the memory that once I would have shrunk from even standing *near* these. I had believed that the toxic print would seep into the air and corrupt my mind. How did Howard do it? Are people that easily tricked? Will they believe anything? The need for Jamie is suddenly like a great wave rolling through me.

Kneeling down, I push my hand in deeper, feeling right to the back of the cabinet. I must check everywhere. If I fail to find the telephone this time it may be weeks—years—before I get another chance. And suddenly I realize I have leant forward too far because the whole cabinet begins to tip towards me. The Outsider papers start sliding and I try to stop them and push them back in but they keep sliding and now there is a thud and a hurried pattering drip. I realize the crystal jar has also tipped, the glass stopper has unstopped, and the gold liquid is running down into the slide of newspapers.

My first panicked thought is to get up and run—to just leave it all here. But with all this evidence it would not be a week or a year I would have to wait before I tried again. It would be beyond Endtime. For ever.

My hands are trembling as I stand the jar back up, using the skirt of my dress to wipe the spillage that is still dripping down the side of the cabinet. It stains yellow. I will have to find a way to get rid of it later. The High Order Followers would have to Unburden if they discovered a stain like this in my washing.

When I have done my best with the drips, I kneel back down to check the Outsider newspapers. The top ones have soaked up the liquid and I dab them frantically with my skirt again. It does not make any difference, except that my skirt becomes smudged with grey. I try to convince myself that the stained papers may not matter. Maybe Howard and Rael never look at them. The newspapers might just be here for some kind of . . . I stop, puzzled. What are they here for? Are there other secrets hidden in them, stories that the Outsider world knows all about, that are Forbidden for us. Things like that meteorite shower?

I scan the front page of the top one. There is a problem with the prices of Outsider houses. An Outsider riot at a place called Glasgow. An Outsider teenager gone missing from home. I suppose Howard and Rael can deceive us better if they are aware of things like this. They can stay ahead of anything we might inadvertently hear, and need to Unburden.

The gold liquid has bobbled the newspaper. As I struggle to flatten it with the heel of my hand, my eye catches something else—two lines in bold print running along the bottom:

CULTWATCH—a double-page special report. Inside information from authentic and up-to-date sources. Our week by week investigation starts today on page 7.

I turn to page 7. I have even forgotten my search for the telephone—it seems that I have to know this, the way Outsiders see us. I want as much Outsider thinking as I can get.

I begin to scan the report, and then freeze.

There is a photograph—black and white and grainy, but I know who it is. I would know him in any form.

> Cultwatch investigator James
> Warner.

I cannot take it in—cannot understand. But it is as if a glass jar in my head has tipped.

> James Warner, the youngest mem-
> ber of the Cultwatch team, has
> gained access to the sinister
> True Cause cult. Warner is not
> at liberty to reveal his source
> as the cult is suspected of carry-
> ing out acts of revenge against
> its members but this young girl--
> one of the cult's Elite--has been
> providing hard-edged information
> that may help Cultwatch expose
> this evil, manipulative group for
> the scam that it is. Cultwatch,

which was formed nine years ago
when . . .

I do not want to read any more. I do not want to
know. He never wanted me—not me for myself. He
wanted to use me to expose True Cause.

He called me beautiful.

He called me beautiful.

I am easily tricked. I will believe anything.

I stare down at the face I have Imaged and
Imaged and Imaged and I have to press my knuckles
against my mouth because there is a sound so
wrenched and so torn that is trying to come out that
if I let it I know that the whole of Hill Park—the
whole farm—maybe the whole world—will hear.

And I am still hunched with my knuckles
against my mouth when Rael walks into the room.

He holds out his hand and smiles at me like a
friend. My only friend. I let him take my hand and
pull me unsteadily to standing.

The Outsider newspaper slides from my liquid-
stained lap and flops down onto the floor.

"Outsiders can be dangerous and devious," he
says softly. "Trust leads to tragedy."

I cannot speak. I can only let him lead me, his
hand gripped tightly on mine, to my room.

32

"There are bad things coming. I can feel it. I can feel it." Howard throws a bowl of marinated peppers across the long white table. He breaks bread and hurls it at the walls. Some of it hits, some of it misses. He throws fruit. He throws pies.

Then he picks up a golden goblet and strides along the line of silent Brides, marking the W sign in blood-red wine on their foreheads.

Except for me. He goes straight past me. Does not even look at me.

I suppose he is angry. I suppose he blames me for whatever he knows is coming. I suppose I will Receive Punishment soon. I do not care. There is nothing in the whole world to care about. I do not

understand who I am or why I even exist. Why anything ever happens. Why anyone ever bothers.

A fogged memory of Meryl pushes out. Her short
cropped hair. Her blank deadened eyes. I do not care.
I do not care.

Later, in the Prediction Practice session, I try to
Image myself strapped to the tree. The Image does
not come. Instead all I can see is the inside of that
car. The ginger-haired man is still driving. The man
with the beard is still beside me. And there is someone else, although it is not my mother. I cannot
Image my mother. And I realize suddenly that I cannot Image her because she is gone. I will never ever
ever see or know my mother again.

I shrug. My eyes stare blank and dead.

Howard is smearing blood-red Ws across the
windows.

I do not care. I do not care.

33

It has taken a week to feel anything. I know it is a week because I have been counting the nights—the great stretch of time when I lie staring up at the ceiling or sometimes sit by the window watching the dark outside.

I do not want Jamie in my head. I want all this thinking to crumble to dust. But the Image of him will not leave me alone.

How could he? How could he?

I stare at the cracks and think about Bronwyn and Katrina and the other Brides and I wish I could be happy. So happy. It must be a thousand times better to be them, than to be me.

I twist suddenly on the soft white bed and grab

the soft white pillow and start hitting it and hitting it. But hitting it is not enough and I grapple with the seams and begin to tear even though I did not know I was this strong. I like this tearing pillow noise. I tear again and again and again. The pillow is filled with soft white feathers that burst out and I realize I am shouting because I have feathers in my mouth.

"It's a Bad Thing—being deceived," a voice says from the doorway. "The knowledge eats at you. It messes with your head."

I drop the rags of what was the pillow and look round.

It is Rael.

"Yes." I still have feathers in my mouth and I pick them out as I stare at his shadowed shape. I remember how he grazed the air with a rope.

"Do you need to Unburden anything more?"

I shake my head. I Unburdened when it first happened. Said everything. "When will I Receive Punishment?"

Rael comes closer and looks down at the shreds of pillow. "It doesn't seem necessary yet," he says.

I feel tired, and lean back on the metal bed-frame. It presses into my back, and it hurts, but I do not care. I do not care.

"Have you considered," says Rael slowly, "that he didn't mean to Betray you?"

"No." I speak slowly too. "I haven't considered that."

"Can you consider it now?"

"He used me." This comes out in a harsh crack, as if the words have been trapped somewhere and have only just found an opening to spring through.

"But he's an Outsider. He doesn't understand the joy and the glory of the things you know."

I stay silent, because I do not understand the joy and the glory of the things I know either.

"Truth is a matter of perception, Elinor. Think round that for a moment."

I think round it, then frown up at him. "I don't know what it means."

"It means the way you look at something shapes what you feel about it. Try to Image things through Outsider eyes."

I try to Image Jamie as someone misunderstanding, but instead he comes through holding my hand. Stroking my hair. "I think he knew."

The harsh crack words have already left me, and my voice is flat and tired.

I wish Rael would go away and leave me alone, but he keeps pushing new thoughts at me. "Perhaps in your Outsider friend's mind, the end will justify the means."

"He thinks Howard is mad." It is a risk saying this, but I cannot bear Rael's strange defence of Jamie. I want to make him stop.

Rael only nods, as if this statement is nothing. "Outsiders think like that."

I make myself Image Meryl and Caroline Markham and the day of the Divine Writings. There are things I would like to ask, but do not dare. Splinters of bark spat and fell as he lashed the rope.

He comes very close, sits beside me on the bed, his milk-pale eyes washing mine. "There are thousands of ways of making sense of the world. Outsiders are all chasing answers." His voice has softened, and I am strangely lulled by it. "Let me paint a few of their answers for you. There's an Order—a group—which exists only for women. These women must shave their hair. Dress in sexless clothes. Rarely if ever see their families. Sexual pleasures are Forbidden, because they've attended a ritual where they get Bonded to their Master—much the same as you Chosen—only there is one main difference. The Master in this case is dead."

"Dead?" I Image the dead Master—stuffed and preserved—propped up at a Bonding ceremony. "That's so strange. Are they happy?"

"They want it. They choose it. And the Outsiders that follow this group revere these women. They believe they are High Order."

I think that not many Outsiders would choose a madness like that. I Image the women living out their strange unhappy lives on a tiny farm, somewhere remote. "How do they run their meetings if their Master is dead?"

"He speaks to them through a select few."

"A bit like the Divine Writings coming to Howard?"

"A bit like the Divine Writings coming to Howard."

I glance sideways at Rael, thinking of what I know about the Divine Writings.

He ignores the glance. "The women are called 'nuns.'" He takes a strand of my hair and twists it as he speaks. "They're part of one of the most powerful religious movements on the Outside."

"Nones." I repeat it slowly. "Nones." I think this is a good name. I think it describes them well.

"So—truth is all a matter of perception, don't you think?" Rael says softly.

I am still struggling to focus on what this means, but I become aware that he is stroking my arm. He has a rough touch, and I would like to ask him to stop, but he gashed a scar down the trunk of that tree. It is best to stay on his side.

"There's this other bizarre belief that after death the soul gets reborn into another body—not just people, but all animals. Can you Image that? Would you follow it?"

I shake my head, grappling with the idea of my soul being reborn in a cow or a sheep. What about birds? Butterflies? Ants?

"There are Outsiders who worship rocks and stones. Beings with many heads. Gods who go for sex. Gods who don't. Gods who hang about on planets waiting for new-born bodies to inhabit . . . trust me when I say that you can take your pick of false beliefs."

"So—" I make myself ask the question, "what is different about True Cause? Why would we be true and all the others false?"

"Our Master is amongst us, isn't he, Elinor? We can see he exists. That's a major difference, don't you agree?"

I nod. I am sure I could not follow a Master who was dead.

"And think of Howard. Why would he put himself through so much torment for a false cause? You've seen his struggles. You must sense the pressure."

I am sensing the pressure. My head is full of this struggle.

"And do you doubt our Followers? Van-loads of New Joiners every week. They're leaving behind all the other choices. Some truth is ringing louder with us, or why would they come?"

His questions swim round my mind. Why would they? Why would they?

Rael is so close I can almost smell his words. "They choose us because of Howard, Elinor. The light is on him. They can see it. They can feel it. You're so lucky to be part of the one True Cause."

I nod. My head is very heavy.

"Let me hear you say it. I want the words. Over and over."

"Lucky. So lucky. Lucky. So lucky." My thoughts begin to slip into old and comfortable grooves. "Howard our Master. Howard who Saves. Lucky. So lucky." Time passes. It could be minutes. It could be hours. "Lucky. So lucky."

"You could rise above all of this, you know." Rael's voice seems to come from a great distance away. Has he just started talking again, or has he been saying things for a long time? I must concentrate. Concentrate. "You could let your Outsider be saved by us. Saved by you."

"I wanted that once." My whispered answer seems to be being dragged out of me. "But he's a Bad Thing. A Bad Thought. Dangerous. Devious. Trust leads to tragedy . . ."

"Only if it's not controlled. Only if it's left to run free. But I'll be watching out for you from now on. I'll never stop watching."

"Never stop watching. Never stop watching."

"So now that I can see that you understand, I have a task for you. Howard wants you to bring this James Warner to me." I have a dim sense of Rael's eyes still fixed on mine. "He wants to come, but he's scared. Other Outsiders are corrupting his mind, but he's drawn to us—through you. You are the channel he has to swim through. You're the one who can save him."

"I can save him. I can save him."

"If you can give Howard this one thing, you'll have Forgiveness. No punishment. No pain. Only the joy and the glory of what you've done for your Master."

"The joy and the glory. The joy and the glory."

Rael pulls me to standing and leads me to the window. Dawn is coming, the sky washed pink and the air full of birds who sing as sweetly as those in the glass room. Truth is a matter of perception.

"He's out there somewhere—Unsaved—and Endtime could hit us at any moment. We've got to find a way to reach him, haven't we? You can see that, can't you? We've got to come up with something that won't make him feel as if we're setting a trap."

There is just one last star flickering in the sky. Saving Jamie is the right thing. I am lifted by this thought. Elated by it. Truth is a matter of perception. The end justifies the means.

A number floats into my head, glowing like gold. Like treasure. Something of his. Something unique. "I know a way . . ." I say.

34

He should be here by now. I am trying to ignore the knots in my stomach which are making me feel sick. It must only be months, but it feels like years since I was here with him. The smells unsettle me. The dark moist wood. Fungus and moss and old leaves.

It takes me back to memories I do not want to have. Bad Thoughts. Bad Thoughts. His voice hurt me. I had expected a squashed-up sort of voice, as if being inside a mobile telephone would somehow alter the sound; but although the voice crackled, I could tell it was his. Unique.

My own unique voice was stiff and careful as I said, "Jamie. Hello."

There was a pause, and then he said, "Elinor?"

He sounded warm. So warm. Dangerous and devious. Dangerous and devious.

"I wanted to talk to you." Rael had told me to say that. We Role Played it. Role Played a range of Jamie's possible responses, and ways to get him to agree to meet me. Rael tried to inspire me with Sudden Sight, too, but nothing came. Only the inside of that car again.

But in the end it was Jamie who suggested the meeting. "Oh, Christ. I want to talk to you, too. You don't know how much I've been . . . but look—let's not talk now. Not on the phone. Can we meet?"

"In the woods?" I brightened my voice as if I had only just thought of the idea. "I could get away tomorrow morning. Ten o'clock."

"I'll be there." There was another pause, then, very softly, "Are you okay?"

"I . . . I'll tell you when I see you." I gave no clue that I was happy. I had Role Played that with Rael too. He made me see that Outsiders are drawn to bad news—not good. *Evil Cult Flogs Failing Followers. Mad Messiah Molests Child Brides.* I had to make Jamie believe that it was me that needed saving, and not him.

"See you at ten," he said. "Take care."

Take care. Take care.

He should be here by now.

Unless—unless somehow I have missed him.

It feels terrible, this sudden thought that he might already be gone.

Rael will be angry. And Jamie will not be saved.

I will not let these thoughts spill through my head. I must keep waiting. Must keep waiting.

The fallen trunk is sprouting fresh growth, as if it does not understand that the tree's life has ended. I think how brave nature is. How determined to survive. The new leaves curl upwards towards the light, covering the hollow where Jamie stashed the pasties that day. I wish the Jamie memories would turn to crumbs, but they are fresh growth on dead wood.

I shiver and pull the shawl tighter around my bare shoulders. These bride dresses were never meant for outdoors.

Picking a stick from the ground I stroke the new leaves. They tremble and bend sideways, exposing the hollow. Jamie hid his food in here before. A new thought jolts my mind. Maybe he did not feel safe waiting exactly here. Maybe he is nearby, but out of sight. Maybe he has left me a secret note that tells me where to look.

I trace the hollow's rotten edge and scratches of bark fall away. I push the stick further inside—and stop. I am touching something soft. Some sort of small animal. Shrinking back, I feel half scared and half worried. Scared it might come snarling out at me. Worried I might have hurt it. I try to think what sort of creature would huddle inside a tree. Maybe a squirrel or a fox? Whatever it is it does not do the snarling thing. It stays very still.

It is dead. It must be. I lean closer, a part of me now prepared for something rotten or crawling with maggots, but there is no smell and no movement. Whatever it is, it has not been dead for long.

I must not look. I need to concentrate. Concentrate. Rael will be waiting back at Hill Park. There is no room for mistakes.

He should be here by now. He should be here by now.

And then suddenly I think that I cannot just not know what sort of creature it is, and I part the leaves with my stick one more time, craning to look inside.

It is not very big—dark brown. Quite furry. I decide it must be a dog because of the type of brown it is, and I wonder what happened to make it slink in here to die. But as I keep looking I think suddenly that it is not a dog, it is not anything real. It is some sort of soft toy. Puzzled about what child would have even been in these woods, let alone choose to hide a toy in here, I lift the soft brown lump of it with the stick. And now I see what it is, but I cannot believe it. And even when I begin to believe it, I still cannot understand.

A soft brown ear. A soft brown paw. Gruffles.

35

I am sitting on the fallen tree, clutching Gruffles and remembering.

There was a boy. I cannot quite Image his face but I get the sense that I liked him. I liked him a lot. He lived up the road with his dad, David. They used to stay over and we sometimes went for days out together, all four of us. We sat on the beach and ate ice creams. One afternoon the boy made me a sand-castle and we watched the sea fill the moat before crumbling the soft walls away. The boy taught me to swim that day. David told funny stories to my mum and once he buried her legs in sand while she slept. When she woke up she laughed in a free, shining way that was new for her, and chased him down to the sea. The boy grabbed my hand and we raced after them. The water was warm and white waves washed us, making us shout. When I looked further out, towards the horizon, all of the sea was silver. I was happy. So happy.

It was the boy who gave me the present. He had wrapped it untidily in bright balloon wrapping. When I tore at the paper I saw a soft brown ear. A soft brown paw. As I pulled the bear out of the wrapping I smiled up at the boy. "Thank you. He's beautiful."

The boy looked a bit embarrassed, but he shrugged and grinned back. "Happy birthday, Ellie." He had moss-green eyes. Very warm.

36

We could leave each other messages. If things get too desperate, I'll put some sort of code in here, and wait for you in the road.

The memory shuffles forward as if it has been waiting, curled tight and listening behind curtains.

Gruffles is the message. A sort of code. Jamie has put him there because he hopes I will understand, and I do.

I know what is going to happen.

I even know where I have to be.

I have seen it—Imaged it—in the Prediction Practice sessions, although it has meant nothing until now. I suppose I should be Elated because Prediction Practice has worked for me at last, but this is not the moment for joy. It is the moment for the clearest thinking I have ever done. I am not saving Jamie. Jamie is saving me. He is out there, on the road. He will already be waiting.

But I must take care. Great care.

Rael has said he has warned off the Watchers, because we must not make Jamie suspicious, but Rael is dangerous and devious so I cannot be sure. My task was to talk to Jamie, to be warm to him, but to keep a tremor in my voice. That way he would think that there were things I was afraid to reveal. He would think there was more he could find to expose us with.

And once I was sure he was desperate to unravel the rest, I would invite him inside the mansion. "A secret back entrance." I had Role Played whispering this. "I've got things—difficult things—I need you to see." He would go with me, of course—how could he not? And then, once he was inside, Rael would be waiting.

Rael did not crowd me with further details. He said there was nothing more I needed to know. All that mattered was that my task would be over. I could immerse myself in True Cause and be happy. So happy.

As he said this he locked me with his milk-pale

eyes, his hand squeezing mine. Almost crushing it. "You're doing a Good Thing," he said.

Truth is a matter of perception. Maybe happiness too.

Take care. Great care.

I reach the stream and walk along the boggy edge, aware of every slush and squelch. Twigs catch my hair and my dress has been badly snagged by brambles. I cannot manage this mud in the strappy white shoes so I slip them off and go barefoot. If anyone is following my footprints are as good as arrows.

I am near the road. I can see the line of our fence with its tight metal mesh and barbed top. I press against the nearest tree. Once I go over to the fence, I will have to act fast. Jamie said there was a "dodgy bit"—not much but enough—only it is nowhere obvious. I wonder how long Rael will wait before he gets suspicious.

Flitting to the next tree, and then the next, I look frantically. Nothing. Nothing. I rub my hands down the tree. "Howard says you can talk. Tell me what you know. Tell me where he gets in," I whisper.

The wind teases the leaves in the cage of branches above me, but the tree stays silent.

I sink down slowly to the ground. I cannot go

forward, but I will not go back. I will huddle here for ever and everything that is me will slowly crumble away and be buried in the mulch of leaves.

Maybe one day somebody will find the mound left behind, and mark their forehead with the dust.

Somebody mad. Somebody like Howard.

I lean my head against the trunk and wonder how long it will be before I am found. And it is then that I see it—a distortion along the base of the mesh, as if it has been pulled and then put back. I could easily have missed it, and I would never have spotted it from a standing position. This is real Elation. Golden and Glorious. I crawl forward on my stomach, Gruffles still clutched in my right hand, easing my way across the damp ground. My dress is just rags, my hands sticky with mud, my hair caught up with moss and twigs.

He called me beautiful.

For a moment, I almost laugh.

The mesh is stiffer than I had expected. I push my hands through first and then, lying my cheek on the ground, grip clumps of grass on the other side. Panting, wriggling, I pull myself underneath. Sharp points of wire scratch into my back. The dress catches. It tears so easily. There will be nothing left once I get through. If I get through. And suddenly I *am* through, half dazed, clutching Gruffles and the rags of my dress, and wondering which way to run.

But in the next instant the car is there, swerving up onto the verge, the passenger door thrown open. "Quick. Now!" Jamie grabs me, bundling me in between him and the bearded man. And I realise I know this bearded man. David. Jamie's Dad. In the driver's seat the same ginger-haired man is screeching us away. The speed overwhelms me, and I fight not to panic.

Either side of me the world is a blur.

I think that any minute a black Mercedes will roar up behind us.

What have I done? What have I risked?

And then Jamie takes my hand, touches my hair, my shoulder, as if he cannot believe I am really here. "I didn't know if all this would work." His voice is tight and strained, as if he has been somewhere he would never want to go again. "But it was the best we could think of. We've been planning it ever since you rang."

I nod, although I do not dare to speak. If I spoke, I would cry and if I cry I may never stop.

The car has turned towards the town, settling into a less desperate speed. Soon we are driving through Braxbury, familiar buildings flashing past. I keep my head down in case there are any Followers out Spreading the Word, shivering as it hits me that I may never be properly free.

"You must be cold." David twists out of his jacket and lays it over me, tucking it round as if I am a child in bed. I glance sideways at him although I am scared to look properly. I am scared of everything. In the sideways glance I take in that the beard is grey now. I wonder if I would have recognized him if I had seen him in the streets.

"You'll have to try and trust us." He is smiling. "I know this whole thing feels crazy, but it's the only way to beat them."

"I rescued Gruffles for you, hoping I could get him back to you one day," Jamie adds. "I found him in your house—Dad had a key and we went round, worried, because we couldn't get hold of you."

"Although I guessed what had happened," David shakes his head slowly. "Maria and I had argued about True Cause enough times before. Still—it was lucky me and Jamie went when we did. A day later, and the place was gutted. Stripped out by Followers. Gruffles would've wound up in one of the car boot sales, along with most of the other small and less expensive stuff."

I still cannot speak, but I can remember. I can

remember crying as my mother took Gruffles from me. She was very calm. Very certain. "Possessions weigh you down," she'd said.

The ginger man speaks for the first time. "We hoped the bear would be the trigger you needed. Jamie told me you never let it out of your sight after he gave it to you." He glances back over his shoulder. "I get called in to de-programme a lot of Followers, and I had a gut feeling the bear would work for you. Everyone's breaking point is different, and I work on instinct as much as anything . . ."

"That's Martin, our de-programmer. He's been with Cultwatch from the start." Jamie squeezes my hand and nods towards the ginger man.

"I've helped people get free of all sorts of cults and sects and weird movements—but your lot . . . that Howard . . ." He gives a long low whistle. ". . . It always takes a long time."

I look at the back of Martin's head. I am not sure what he is talking about, but it is so strange that I Imaged him. Dreamt about him. And now he is here.

Jamie is still talking. "We've been working towards some sort of rescue ever since an ex-Follower stumbled into our offices. She got dumped. The great Master Howard does that a lot with Followers who aren't 'useful' anymore. The girl let me interview her for a newspaper article—she's in one of our hostels now. When she described you— her one-time Shadow as she called you—we went a bit nuts with excitement."

"I didn't think we stood much chance," David interrupts him, "but I didn't know the risks my son was prepared to take to find you. I didn't know he'd made contact until you rang him yesterday, and if I'd known he was sneaking about in Hill Park wood I'd have locked him in the office and thrown away the key."

"I knew that. That's why I kept my mouth shut." Jamie squeezes my hand again. "But I reckoned I had a chance. The first time I got in I was only going to make a few notes, just to try and get the layout of the place . . . and then you showed up and it was like a gift. I couldn't waste it. We've been desperate to find you for a long, long time."

I sit staring out through the windscreen, the whole of Outside rushing at me. So Meryl was Ejected.

And it was not me that Jamie had drawn from in his article—it was her. I was not Betrayed.

And all these Outsiders have been working to help me.

It is hard for me to take this in. I feel I have been

standing in a cold dark place not knowing that only two steps away and out through a hidden door the sun was shining. There are tears stinging my face and I wipe them away with Gruffles's soft brown body. He smells like he used to smell, although the blue ribbon has frayed and faded.

A long long time. A long long time.

I suppose there is a lot of filling in to do.

37

Today I am going to wear a green skirt and a shirt. A green shirt. A Wednesday shirt. Nobody knows about my Wednesday shirt. Or my Thursday jumper. Or my Friday dress. They see me wearing them, but so far they have not noticed that I am keeping with True Cause colours. Perhaps they never will. I have to keep quiet about these things.

But at least I have stopped that sick knotted feeling in the mornings when I slide open the wardrobe door. All the clothes Naomi bought me—Outsider clothes. So many colours and patterns and fabrics and lengths.

She bought me trousers, too—jeans—but I have never worn them. I cannot believe I will ever want to wear jeans.

Martin says it will take a long time, although even he does not know that I have so many Bad Thoughts.

They are all trying so hard.

I pull on the skirt, button up the Wednesday shirt, and straighten the primrose yellow bed sheet. All this room is primrose yellow. Primrose yellow curtains. A primrose yellow lampshade. The rest of the house is a muddle of colour, which Naomi says is "typical blokes," but they did the primrose yellow for me.

I am lucky. So lucky.

I go down the wooden slatted stairs, although I avoid the front room. The television is in the front room. Instead I head for the kitchen.

Jamie and David are out—they go to Cultwatch every day. It is their job. Their mission. I think about Howard's mission, which is the opposite to theirs. I wonder if having a mission is a Good Thing. A reason for being. I cannot believe that I will ever have one. "Being" in itself seems hard enough to me.

I have never been to the Cultwatch office, although Jamie drives me to see Meryl at their hostel sometimes. We never say much. We just hold hands and hug. Meryl cannot cope with Outside yet, although Martin does a lot of Counselling with her.

It will take a long time.

It will take a long time.

They have not found out what happened to Isabel, but Jamie says it is likely she will have been dumped a long way away, and is probably living rough somewhere. I hope he is right that she is actually somewhere. I hope he is right that she is living. When I feel strong enough, I will try to find her. I will not give up on her. I will not let her down.

They have never found out what happened to my mother—Maria—either. Jamie says that my memory was very sharp—the memory of that day when I hid behind the curtains and watched Martin try to break her from the True Cause way. But after that it was as if she disappeared from my life—and from the world. Jamie said that they tried and tried to gain some word of her, but she had gone without a trace. Rael would probably have seen to that. He would have sent her somewhere secret—they had places if they needed them. They would have wanted her away from me. And now, even if Cultwatch did discover her, it would be too late. After all this time, they might force back her body, but they would never reawaken her mind. This thought makes me sad, and sorry, but at least Jamie has been honest.

I open the fridge door. There is cheese and bread

and yoghurt and pasties and puddings and pies. The sick knotted feeling starts up again.

I would have liked rice.

I take some bread and eat it dry, even though Jamie always tries to make me put a spread on it. He does not push me though. He does not push me with anything.

Not even kissing. Although we do that—sometimes. Very gently, when David is not around. But Jamie says we must not rush anything. He says I am going through enough.

I am troubled by the noises in this Outsider house. It is full of sound. The fridge hums. Pipes sometimes knock and bang. From time to time there is the sudden screech of the telephone.

Jamie has trained me to answer the telephone because he is worried about my being here on my own. The person who telephones me most is Naomi. She visits a lot too. Naomi has shown me Outsider ways to have my hair, and has even asked me to go out to a Drinking Den with her. She says she has been Jamie's friend since they went to school together, and any friend of his is a friend of hers.

I may go one day. I have not said "no." But it will take a long time. It will take a long time.

There is a talking box—a radio—in the kitchen

and I have grown brave enough to listen to it when the day feels too long. The radio is black with dials and switches and a tiny screen that lights up when I press the "on" button. Jamie has taught me about the "on" button, although it still makes me jump every time the voices start. I keep the sound very low, and Jamie has found something called a "local channel" where the music does not do anything to startle me. Nothing bad has happened to me from listening to the radio, and sometimes I just sit by it and turn it on and off. On and off. I feel strange when I do that, but excited. Like the way I felt when I went with Isabel to look for snowdrops, and I wanted to swing and stretch my hands.

I remember things like that so much more easily now.

Today there is a singing voice inside the radio.

It is a woman, and she is singing about a Moon River. I Image this Moon River, which flows silver in my mind. The song is soft and drifts with dreams and hearts that swirl down my Moon River, down to a sea full of stars. I have the bread in one hand and I sit on a wooden kitchen chair, leaning my head back and closing my eyes. I am floating floating.

It is like the chants in Star Temple, the way we all held hands and swayed. There are things that I miss, although I know this is a Bad Thought. A Bad Thought. Suddenly the Moon River singing stops.

"We are interrupting this programme to bring you a report regarding a number of bodies which have been discovered at Hill Park mansion, home of the controversial cult leader Howard Reiki. According to a police spokesperson the bodies, which are believed to have been gassed, are those of Howard Reiki himself and fifteen unidentified young women. The discovery was made after several of the Followers became concerned when their Master did not emerge from what they had been advised would be a week-long meditation session held in a special sealed room at the top of the house.

Police are also concerned as to the whereabouts of Rael Rampton, who is known to have acted as Adviser and Chief Bodyguard to Howard Reiki. It has been revealed that a significant amount of the cult's funds were withdrawn from a Swiss bank account just over a week ago . . ."

I turn the radio off. On off. On off.

On off.

On off.

I do not know what the voice in it is saying anymore.

On off.

On off.

On off.

On off.

The telephone screeches and my hand is shaking as I pick it up. It is hard to keep it steady enough to hold to my ear.

"Ellie . . . ?" Jamie's unique voice. "I'm on my way back. Something's happened."

"I know. I heard the radio."

"I'm sorry, sweetheart. I know you must be going through it. It must have been a terrible way to die. Just hang on for me. I'll be as quick as I can."

I do not answer. Cannot answer.

Putting the telephone back on its cradle, I walk to the kitchen window and stare out at the Outsider garden.

I know what room they died in. I can see the whole scene in my head. I Image Rael, too, sitting in that swivel chair, controlling the gas flow on the flaming torches like he did the day I was Enlightened. The Image comes through clear and crisp. Is this Sudden Sight?

I am wondering . . . wondering. Rael is dangerous and devious. I think he may be capable of anything. But is this something the Outsider police would ever be able to prove? And how much does it matter?

In my head I Image Howard leading the Brides into the room. A terrible way to die. A terrible way to die. But suddenly I am not so sure. For Jamie, yes. For all Outsiders. For me, too, probably. But for them—if they died beside Howard they would have been happy. So happy. And they had probably believed they were Transcending—like the Ecutarusians. Howard must have believed it too. Rael could control him as easily as he could control that flow of gas. Truth is a matter of perception. Maybe happiness is too.

I am tasting salt, and realize I have entered the State of Sorrow. I press my fingers against my closed eyelids as if I might somehow push all this silent grief back in, but it will not stop seeping out of me. I open my eyes again, but I cannot see clearly. A small blurred shape hops across the hazed garden, and it is a moment before I realize it is a blackbird, pecking at the lime-green grass with its yellow beak.

And suddenly I understand something new. The birds in the glass room have no choice but to be in those cages. The Brides had no choice but to be with Howard. And it hits me that *that* is the difference between True Cause and Outside. It is not what is right or what is wrong—it is having the choice. And being able to use it.

The day outside is a sharp, heated blue. There are bushes and trees, and their branches stretch and spread. The sunlight filters the leaves, dazzling some and shading others. I had not known there were so many greens. There are other colours too. Pink flowers and lilac flowers and shouting red. It is as if I am seeing colour for the first time ever.

I turn suddenly, running upstairs and tearing off the Wednesday green. I grab a peach pink top. A green jacket. And jeans.

The jeans are stiff, like wearing cardboard, but I force them on and I am just struggling with the button when Jamie comes in—over to me—his arms tight round me.

"I'm sorry, sweetheart. Dad and Martin have gone up there with a stack of Social Workers. The police reckon it's a nightmare. None of the Followers know what the hell to do . . ."

I press my head into his shoulder, and Image the Followers. Are they crying? Chanting? Hugging? What is Imogen doing? Felicity? Little stick-thin Gabriella? For all of them it will be worse than an exploding ball of fire or the earth splitting or a giant wave racing in from the sea.

I draw back from Jamie. "I need to go there. I can talk to them. Help them . . ."

"The police won't . . ."

"They will. If you explain."

He looks at me for a long time. "Me and Dad
lost it when you and Maria went. It was why we s
Cultwatch. It was all done for you. This bit—wl
happened between you and me—that's been a bon
but the main thing was always to get you away . . . if y
go back up there you might get drawn into it again . .

I shake my head because I know everything wi
be all right. I have already Imaged what will happe
next. "Howard's gone. Rael's gone. Without them
True Cause has crumbled to dust. But I'll be able to
help. I'll call a meeting in Star Temple. I'll reassure
all the Followers. Tell them what to do next. They'll
listen to me and gradually . . . gradually . . . they
might start to listen to you." I am talking very fast,
taking his hand, pulling him back down the stairs,
noticing but not minding the cardboard stiff jeans.

"But . . ."

"Trust me," I say. "I'm thinking for myself."
Thinking for myself. Thinking for myself.

And as we run out to Jamie's car and squeal away
up the road towards Hill Park, I know that however
terrible this moment is, these are Good Thoughts.

♦